# Divorce *Not* Granted

ADOLFO RUDY GELSI

INK START MEDIA
265 Eastchester Dr Ste 133 #102
High Point NC 27262

# Divorce *Not* Granted

ADOLFO RUDY GELSI

# PREFACE

My name is Adolfo Rudy Gelsi. I prefer to be called Rudy. Since I was a little boy, everyone in my family has called me Rodolfo. When I came to America about fifty years ago, all my friends started to call me Rudy, an English way of closeness.

I write about life. I have always had a passion to write about anything that comes to mind. I love to write at night while everyone else is sleeping. The confusion of daytime takes away the sensibility of my thoughts. This is a love story.

# AUTHOR·S NOTE

## THE STORY

I met a beautiful young woman on a train to New York. We left from Bridgeport, an industrial city located in southern Connecticut. It is one of the biggest industrial cities in America.

The train station was full of people. It seemed like everyone was going to New York that day. It was a sunny day. The temperature must have been in the 70s. I went to the bar in the station to get a drink. Just as I sat down, the whistle blew announcing the arrival of the train to New York. I was worried about finding a seat when the train arrived.

I was one of the last people to get on. I walked through the cars in search of a seat. Finally in the last car I saw a beautiful woman sitting by herself. I politely asked her if the seat was taken. She looked at me with a lovely voice, she told me to sit. The train was going very slowly and would stop at every station. I tried to read the paper but it was too noisy.

I would love to start a conversation with the young woman, but the difference in age is too great. I can tell she is very shy. Her eyes were tired and red. She held a handkerchief to dry her tears that occasionally would wet her face. I looked at her for a while and with bravery, I asked her if everything was okay. She looked at me and without hesitation, she said; "Do you want to know why I am crying, why I am so sad? Would you believe that yesterday I got married and my husband left me after the reception? He is a soccer player and today he has to fly to a Paris for a very important game. I hope that after the game I will see him and be able to spend the first night of our marriage together." I listened and tried to comfort her. Finally, the train arrived at the station in New York and I wished her good luck. She thanked me and left in a hurry. I hope that the beautiful woman is full of happiness. If she reads this play, remember that I was the first man in her life to console her after her marriage.

DIVORCE
NOT
GRANTED

# CAST

(IN ORDER OF APPEARANCE)

Frances

Teresa

Sal Corini

Lio Bard (father of Pamela)

Pamela Pite

Greg Pite

Sue Bard (mother of Pamela)

Attorney Conti

Rachael (baby star)

The Waiter

Renee

The Old Man

Mrs. Dion

Diane (the housekeeper)

Mr. Dion

# ACT ONE

**Scene:** An elegant suite, with at least twenty vases of flowers that embellish the suite. A table from Louis XIV is full of gifts, another full of refreshments. There are four doors leading to other rooms. A large window looks out on the beauty of the garden.

**Frances:** (She is alone in the room observing the display of the gifts. A lot of beautiful gifts she has replayed. She opens a gift to find a fur coat inside. She puts it one and observes herself in the mirror.) This is made just for me! I think that the foolish Pamela is a lucky lady. (She is caught by Teresa who just came in.)

**Teresa:** Good morning, dear!

**Frances:** Good morning, my friend. It is so nice to see you, always elegant!

**Teresa:** Thank you. I do not deserve such a compliment from you.

You look so astonishing in that new fur.

**Frances:** (Takes off the fur and puts it back in the box.) It's not mine.

It is a gift for the wedding. Lots of beautiful gifts.

**Teresa:** (Playing stupid, she already sees the gift.) Oh, that, beautiful gifts.

**Frances:** We always seem to meet a special occasion like Clara's engagement party and Anna Maria's wedding.

**Teresa:** I hope this is for good luck, dear.

**Frances:** About you; you do not think to get married! (A noise from the outside stops Frances from continuing to talk.) Oh! There they are! The wedding party is here. Hurry, call the other guests. She urges Teresa to do so.) Lots of guests enter the big suite. (Frances comes back to the window. Teresa follows.) Look at Greg, very beautiful.

**Teresa:** What a beautiful bride. That white dress. She looks like an angel. She is beautiful.

**Frances:** I don't think she is so beautiful. The dress, the veil, the flowers. I believe any woman adorned like that is beautiful. Pamela is very stupid and that goes for Greg too. He is so eccentric. I don't like him. I think the only beautiful thing he has is his name.

**Teresa:** A young man like Greg who is wealthy and pleasant. I do not think Pamela could have done better than that.

**Frances:** Oh! I don't believe that I would accept to spend the rest of my life with him. I think very different. I would never smell liberty. (To Teresa) I could have lots of men who want me. I let them dream!

**Teresa:** If I were you, I would stop criticizing other people. I tell you as a friend. Even you start to get old; the time passes for everybody. You will not stay young forever; the wrinkles start to show in your body. (She doesn't give Frances' time to respond.) Hurry!! Let's go meet the wedding party. (Frances and Teresa exit. The wedding party starts to enter.)

**Sal:** (Quickly enters the suite; always elegant, he goes straight to the mirror. He looks and starts to talk to himself.) Sal, poor Sal! You are all by yourself, you lost Pamela! No more hope, you are alone. Your heart is broken!

**Lio:** (Enters the suite) Dear Sal, thank you for coming. You are a true friend, a gentleman. I would swear that you would be here even though your heart is broken. I do not know where to start on this joyful day. My daughter has to be happy on this day of her wedding! Thank you, thank you, thank you for the beautiful gift!

**Sal:** I didn't send any gift, just some flowers because we are friends!

**Lio:** I knew it. Sooner or later the truth comes out. From you I didn't expect a lot. I feel like you are in the family. (Lio dries his forehead with a handkerchief and leaves the stage.)

**Sal:** (Goes back to look at himself in the mirror. The guests start to come in and take their places in their seats.) I am good looking. I don't care what everybody says. I have started to get old but still look as if I were twenty years old.

**Pamela** ... Pamela ... whom I love so much ... you left me, you abandoned me. You left me for a soccer player. This is This is horrible ... it is horrible ... this new generation!

**Teresa:** (Enters the suite with a tray full of pastries and goes to Sal.) What's going on, my dear friend, what is it that makes you so upset? Do not think about today as a holy day, I'm here. Eat a pastry. I brought you the ones you like. I know your taste more than anyone else.

**Sal:** (Helps himself to a few pastries.) Thank you! (Gives a sigh of relief with a breath.) Oh! This pastry is like medication, takes away all my bad thinking.

**Teresa:** Please sit down. If you like you can stay by yourself or I can keep you company.

**Sal:** No! My dear, do what you have been doing. It is nice to help on this beautiful day. I'm sure someone will give you credit for helping out. To tell you the truth, I'm depressed. This wedding makes me so mad. To see Pamela and Greg getting married annoys me very much. I can't help it. I can't help it! I don't know what to do to put them apart.

**Teresa:** My dear friend. If I can do anything to alleviate your pain, or the pain in your heart, please do not hesitate to ask. I am here at your disposal.

**Sal:** Thank you, my dear friend. If I need anything, I will ask you.

You can go now. Try to be a good hostess for all the people present at this wedding.

**Teresa:** I can't leave you alone now! You are too agitated.

**Sal:** I would say nervous! Excuse my sincerity . . . really nervous.

**Teresa:** I will stay and keep you company. I never leave one of my friends alone in a difficult moment . . . remember, just friends . . .

**Sal:** If you try to calm me down, I can just tell you it won't work. I am too nervous now. I really believe that not even a tranquilizer could keep me calm.

**Teresa:** I think you are right, my friend, right. . .

**Sal:** It's impossible to heal my heart. The wound is too deep.

**Teresa:** In that case, I have to stay near you. I can't leave you alone.

**I** will be your personal nurse.

**Sal:** Please, my friend! Do not joke about my feelings. I am not in mood!

**Teresa:** But why? I do not really understand. Why have an anchor for a woman like Pamela? She has been teasing you all her life. She believes she can take my Greg away from me and she did. I will be honest with you. I personally detest Greg and always have. I do not like his ways. He was the one who was in love with me.

**Sal:** The truth is that you would marry Greg in a flash, no questions asked! You still savor his sweat, but he chose Pamela to be his wife.

**Teresa:** I assure you that Greg was never my type. I swear. He was the one who came to my house every day. Yes, we were friends, just friends and nothing else. It was there that he me Pamela, and it was there that he started to flirt with her to make me jealous. He thought he was making me jealous! That is not true. I never respected him as a real man.

**Sal:** I believe you and I have both sunk in the same pond of water. But tell me why it was so necessary to invite Pamela when Greg was at your house.

**Teresa:** Are you trying to say that I favored the encounter between Pamela and Greg? You are mistaken, my friend. Think positive. Pamela could never have been your wife. She is so dynamic, athletic. Her mentality is so far advanced that I'm sure if she were to marry you, she would have an affair with another man. I know her very well. Listen to me. Do not despair, you haven't lost much.

**Sal:** I would like to get even with her so she would never forget about me.

**Teresa:** Please do not get mad. I think that the best revenge is to forget about her. I have a suggestion for you. Go out and court some other beautiful girl. Actually, you do not have to go far. Start to court me. I am right next to you. I can assure you that I have a special way to appreciate your compliments. I believe, my dear friend, that you haven't forgotten that beautiful night we spent together when your beautiful friend Pamela went on vacation in Italy? You spent a lot of time with me. If you remember, we both love music. How many times did we go to the theater and piano concerts and talk about the performers? And you, with the magic words of a conductor, spoke to me. Do you remember when you told me that the note was so powerful it induced your soul into mine? To take away the loneliness from your soul.

**Sal:** Yes, that is the truth. You are right!

**Teresa:** I remember that when our bodies were together, we made love for hours without stopping. Then Pamela came. Beautiful I can't deny, but very different for you. I do not understand why the sentiment for love.

**Sal:** Pamela, it gives me this new sensation, new sentiment. She is life, she is dynamic. At the same time, she is very sweet and full of fragrance. Today is the most beautiful day of her life being married to that gay Greg. Please tell me what should I do. To be honest, I don't even know why they invited me to the wedding.

**Maybe** she likes to play with my sentiment. I swear, my dear Teresa, she will pay very dearly. You can bet on it.

**Teresa:** Pamela, she always did take advantage of you. Let's stop now. The wedding party is here. (She points at Pamela and Greg.) They come directly our way. Let them believe that we are very happy for them. This is the best revenge.

**Sal:** My dear, I can pretend that I don't care, but you know this is not the truth. I love Pamela. (Looks at her.) She is full of life.

**Teresa:** She is no different from any other woman. Let's be realistic.

**To** me she is worthless. Let's watch ourselves. We are being Observed.

**Sal:** Really! Who cares? Tell me what I have to talk about. You know that my soul is in turmoil. It is not so easy to forget.

**Teresa:** I'll listen! Talk for God's sake, just keep talking. Say whatever you want, but talk. We have to have our revenge.

**Sal:** (Makes gestures with his hand.) You are a terrified woman. I have too much style for a woman like you. My armory is my patience. I take care of my matters very fast. I am tireless … but Pamela marrying Greg I can't accept. It makes me unreasonable, lights up my anger . . . .

**Teresa:** I know! It is a strong feeling. Dear words for a love you lost. (Pamela and Greg are now greeting the people who came to the wedding.) Why can't you give me the love you have left inside yourself?

**Sal:** My love is immense, extends to infinity.

**Pamela:** (Almost near Sal and Teresa talking. Listening to the last phrase, she gets close.) My dear friend! Teresa, how is everything going? If what I just heard is true, maybe the next wedding will be yours.

**Teresa:** I am so confused. This wedding is so elaborate. (The guests speak in a chorus manner.) Long live the newly-weds! Hurray! (All the guests clap their hands.)

**Pamela:** This is for both of you too. (She turns to the guests.) Please clap your hands for the newly engaged Sal and Teresa, my friends!

**Lio:** (Next to the wall close to a doorway.) Two newly-weds, two newly engaged. (Teresa starts to talk to Greg. Sal and Pamela whisper.)

**Greg:** Listen, Teresa, I am so happy, full of joy that you have finally reached the dream that you always wanted. You know that your happiness is mine. I wish you luck!

**Teresa:** Sal has been asking me to be his wife for a long time, but I am so confused . . . .

**Greg:** Let's go! (He takes Teresa under his arm.) Let's go the bar and toast this happiness you have always wanted!

**Teresa:** I accept with pride. It is a dream every time I am with you.

**Greg:** (On their way to the bar.) Sal! My dear Sal, irresistible as always, even you fell in love. You are a lucky man, you can never find someone as beautiful as Teresa, she is a very lovely lady . . .

(Exiting.)

**Pamela:** (To Sal.) What beautiful words you use. The same words just used with me. I still remember what you used to say. "I will always be your immense love. Your warm welcome . . . . I love you . . . for me you are the only woman in the world, only Pamela, just Pamela. It's Pamela or death." These were your words to me every day. Yes, I am married now, but just a few hours now. I haven't even given my virginity to Greg, and already you start to get close to another woman. If it was somebody else, I wouldn't really care, but Teresa? I never liked that woman. Please, when you talk to her, never talk to like you used to talk to me.

**Sal:** I never loved anyone else the way I loved you. These were the words I was saying to Teresa. My words were about you, Pamela. You know that I only love you and that I will always love you. I am in despair. Why did you get married, why? I would have loved you for the rest of my life. I would kidnap you and take you away. I am the one you should have married. I should have been your husband. . . . don't you understand that I love you.

**Pamela:** I feel privileged by your praise. You know what type of woman I am. I never in a million years would be unfaithful to my husband. No other man in this world could take his place.

**Sal:** As you know, dear Pamela, I have a lot of patience. I will wait.

I love you.

**Pamela:** Sal! I think you are going to have to wait a long time. You will be old, full of wrinkles, and ugly. I think you will be waiting for something that will never happen between me and Greg.

**Sal:** I do not believe it! My intuition tells me that you will be unfaithful to Greg. If there comes a time when he makes you jealous, to be vindictive, you would be unfaithful. I will bet on it. You can save your tears because I know Greg better than you, and I know for a fact that he does not stay with the same woman for a long period of time. He likes to change women as often as he changes his shirt. He can never give you the happiness you deserve.

**Pamela:** Don't be ridiculous! Greg would never be unfaithful to me. Now that we are married, I will stay by his side for the rest of my life. Even when he goes to play in another city, I will follow him. I will give him all my love. I will tell him loving words he will never forget. In his heart I will be the only one. You, my dear Sal Corini, will be remembered as a fanatic with a mouth that would kill any soul. I laugh at the love you have for me .... I be in with you! Never! Do you understand, never!

**Sal:** You can say whatever you want. Just remember I have style. I have more style than Greg ever dreamed. I will never forget that you chose another man in my place. Try to reflect just for a moment. Who is Greg? An athlete who plays soccer. I have news for you, my beautiful Pamela. Greg will not play soccer for a long time. He will eventually get hurt by playing soccer. His future is not so bright. I still don't understand how a beautiful woman like you would marry such a man. He has no style at all. I would never change my image. I have class to give away.

**Pamela:** Good-bye! Elegant man, dreamer. You are full of fantasies that are nonexistent, irresistible man! Good-bye. (She is ready to exit.)

**Sal:** Just a moment! Do not leave like that! Please promise me that for if in any circumstance, if something should happen between you and Greg, you will give me another chance. Remember, I will never stop loving you, never!

**Pamela:** If this is the last thing you want to hear from me and to console your spirit, then I promise. I just hope that Teresa does a good job to help you forget me. Do not feel offended, but I have never liked you. I love only Greg and I am very happy to be his wife. I am sorry, but I have to go now. I can't stay here any longer and listen to these non-sensical words. (Exits.)

**Sal:** (Gets up and goes to the mirror to look at himself.) Yes, it's true that I am close to fifty years old, but I don't look it. That means that I am not fifty! Who cares? Love is blind and shows no age.

**Sue:** (Sees Sal and goes to talk to him.) Hi, my friend.

Congratulations. The word has spread very fast, everybody knows that you are engaged to Teresa. Congratulations again!

**Sal:** What did you say? Please do not repeat that word "engage" again! You are crazy, please! (Looks at the ceiling.) Oh, Donna Carmela, you are the cause of my pain. Greg is the one you always wanted for your daughter. He is the right son-in-law. You and your husband did so much that Pamela had no other choice but to get married to him. I believe she doesn't love him very much. Maybe I should say that the only reason she loves him is that he is an athlete.

**Sue:** Sal! Please. Look in the mirror. Maybe finally you can start to Realize that you are not the right man for my daughter. You two are so different!

**Sal:** You try to imply that I am an old man. You think my idea is silly because of my age? What do you think? How old am I?

**Sue:** How old are you? (Sal keeps looking at the mirror.)

**Lio:** (Enters with a pile of telegrams.) Still more telegrams. Pamela and Greg will be happy to see the manifestation of affect. Not even a day would be time enough to send thank-you notes to all these people. Sal, please sit next to me. Help me read all these telegrams.

**Sue:** This is a good idea! Try to make yourself useful. Do something to be remembered instead of staring into that mirror. The mirror can't talk back you know. It won't tell you if Pamela would have been the right wife for you.

**Sal:** (Sal opens a telegram and reads.) To the newlyweds. Happiness and prosperity for life. Renato Carpi and family. (To Lio.) Do you know these people? (He opens another one.) Greg Pite. This one is for Greg, only Greg. I don't want to be indiscreet and open this one. Maybe it's something personal, maybe something important. What do you think? Do you want to open it?

**Lio:** This one should be important because the chauffeur of the limousine got this one from Greg's house when he went to get the suitcase. Go ahead, open it, and read it to me.

**Sal:** (Opens the telegram and reads the contents.)

**Sue:** Lio, you will go to the station to accompany Greg and Pamela. Don't forget I will come with you when you are ready.

**Lio:** Please Sue! Don't start again. Every time you open your mouth, it looks like you want to start a fight. Don't you remember what Greg said? He doesn't want anyone to accompany him and Pamela to the station. Please do not contradict his will. Especially on a day like today, make him happy. For a change he has all the right in the world to be alone with his wife. He wants some privacy.

**Sal:** Please let's stay calm. Do you want me to read this telegram or what?

**Sue:** Listen, Lio. Greg is right but don't forget that Pamela is my daughter, and to be honest, I don't care what he says. I will go to the station and you will come with me. Now that Greg is married, I will show him what kind of mother-in-law I am.

**Sal:** Please, silence! Please! (Sal starts to read.) "Please join the national soccer team in New York immediately. We leave for Paris. You have to substitute for a player that had an accident. Please leave Bridgeport as soon as you can and please call me." The president of the Soccer Federation.

**Sue:** No! This can't be right. It is impossible that something like this could happen. Greg can't leave his wife now. He can't go to New York and leave for Paris today.

**Sal:** (Goes to the near door.) Greg, Greg, please come here. I have to tell you something.

**Lio:** Calm down, Sue, please stay calm. I don't see what the big deal is. I personally think this is a great honor to represent the USA in the World Cup as a player. Just think the whole world will see him. They can go on their honeymoon after he finishes playing.

**Sue:** Please, Sal. Go try to talk to Greg. I think he will be anxious to take this chance on his wedding day. Let's go. We have to talk to Pamela. I hope everything will be fine. She has been waiting for this day for a long time. She was so excited about going on their honeymoon. (Sue takes Lio by the arm and walks away.)

**Greg:** (Enters the stage.) Sal, did you call me? What's going on? Don't you see I am a very busy man? I am so tired, I must have shaken hands with hundreds of people. I can't wait till this is all over. I want to leave and relax with my beautiful wife, just the two of us.

**Sal:** Please, Greg, read. (Sal gives the telegram to Greg.)

**Greg:** (He takes the telegram and reads to himself.) Oh . . . finally I made it, yes . . . (He smiles.) Yes . . . what a dream to play for the national team! What a dream . . . go to Paris! Play in the World Cup! What a dream that finally came true!

**Sal:** I do not understand why you are so happy. Did you forget that you just got married?

**Greg:** You wouldn't even understand if I told you the feeling, I have but about being called on to play for the national team. This is Dream. Pamela, oh Pamela, I hope you understand. My dream will be your dream. We can go on the honeymoon anytime we want. Sal, if you were a real friend, you would agree with me. But who cares for right now. I have to go to New York to get to the airport. I have to contact the rest of the team. (Talking to Sal.) I would have preferred to stay with Pamela in absolute tranquility for a few days, but I would never have imagined they would call me to play with the best. You have no idea what kind of exposure I will get from being seen by millions of fans.

**Sal:** And Pamela? What are you going to do with Pamela? You forget, she is your wife. You will take her to Paris with you?

**Greg:** What the hell do you mean? My lovely wife . . . forget about her, are you crazy?

**Sal:** Listen, Greg, you know if you take this responsibility to play, you will need to be on top of shape. It will be a big task to represent your country. You must conserve all your energy for this.

**Greg:** Are you trying to insinuate that I can make it? You really believe that I can make it?

**Sal:** The colors of your country are important and easily taken for granted. I personally think if Pamela came with you, she would be a distraction. I suggest the wife stays at home!

**Greg:** You are crazy. You don't know what you are saying. Pamela will come with me. If you don't believe it, then listen. (Greg goes to the phone, gets the phone book, and looks.)

**Sal:** What the hell are you doing? Let that book alone. Don't be so stupid!

**Greg:** You want to know what I am doing? Just watch and you will See.

(Greg dials a number.)

Hello … hello … Travel Agency Sony… Listen, my name is Greg Pite …
yes … Pite, with a P … Pite. I would like to reserve a sleeping car to New
York for tonight … yes, I will wait … thank you ….

(The room is tense. Greg and Sal are very nervous. Greg still
waits at the phone for an answer from the agency.)

Hello … yes … okay. My reservation is confirmed. Thank you, thank you
very much.

**Sal:** You are so stupid! I'm sorry to say it, but you don't know what you
are doing! You are crazy. You will compromise your career, the one you
have been dreaming of for the last five years. You can't just do whatever
you please. At this moment your first thoughts must be for the team. You
will have lots of time to stay with your wife. No! You can't compromise
your future now!

**Greg:** (Looks at Sal with sadness in his eyes, walking with small steps back
and forth.) Sal! You are right! Even you say the right things sometimes.
You are right! But Pamela has to come with me. I will stay next to her. I
swear I won't touch her. We have plenty of time to make love, to feel each
other. My first night with her has to be very special.

**Sal:** Why make it hard on yourself? You know if you take Pamela with
you, you would never be able to resist her body. You would make love to
her for hours. If I were in your place, I know I wouldn't be able to resist.

**Greg:** You will see! I will resist her temptation. The team comes first, then love. Hmm. You are right again. I can't resist her. I want her so badly. But wait a minute. Why are you so worried about all of this?

**Pamela:** Sal: Why? You ask why I'm so worried about you? I'll tell you why. I don't want to see you laughed at by millions of spectators watching the game. I have an idea. If you want Pamela to come with you, why don't you just get two regular seats on the train and not a sleeping car. When you are in Paris, you will have to promise yourself not to sleep with her. You might be able to survive the temptation.

**Greg:** You are unbelievable. You're telling me what I should do on the first night of my wedding. I do not understand. I really do not understand!

**Sal:** I know! The challenge is a very important task. Everybody expects the team to win. If the team does not win, your plays will be criticized. You will get the most criticism of all because you are the substitute. Listen, Greg, I think we are wasting our time. We are talking and talking but not going anywhere. This is a very important decision you have to make. I talk to you as a friend, not a rival for a love lost. You have to make a decision. You will never get another opportunity like this. You have to get serious now. Do you want to be a serious athlete or a lover for a night?

**Greg:** (Interrupts Sal.) You are a really good friend. You really do care about my career. I have to make a decision, time is short. It won't be easy, but I have to make a decision....

**Sal:** I know. I can see your blood boiling. Calm down, my friend ... calm down ... everything will be okay. Just stay calm.

**Greg:** I have decided! It sounds strange, but I think I have a Resolution.

(Greg gets the phone and dials a number.)

Hello! Travel Agency Sony . . . listen, my name is Greg Pite . . . yes . . . Pite with a capital P . . . such a simple name. I can't understand these people, they go to college, and they can't even spell a simple word . . . yes . . . the reason I call . . . a few minutes ago, I called and made a reservation for me and my wife for a sleeping car with the train to New York, yes . . . if it is possible, I would like to make another reservation on the other sleeping car; please try to help me . . . okay, I'll wait thank you, thank you very much . . . you have . . . thanks you again. I will send my driver to get the ticket.

**Sal:** I do not understand anything! Would you like to explain to me what the hell you are doing? Take your time, calm . . . if I understand, you just made another reservation. Who is the other person coming with you and Pamela?

**Greg:** My wife will come with me; yes, she will come. I will never leave without her, not even on a day as special as our wedding. I assure you that I will stay away from the beautiful body. I will make a sacrifice . . . (Greg goes next door and calls.) Papa Lio . . . Mom Sue . . . Pamela, please come here. I have to talk with all of you. (Pamela is ready to leave. She has changed her clothing ready to go on the trip.)

**Pamela:** Greg! My love, what is it? (Get close and kisses him.) Sue: Any good news, my dear son-in-law?

**Greg:** Yes! You will come with us to New York, my dear mother-in- law! You can tell that I love you, my dear old lady.

**Sue:** you are crazy. Yes, you are really crazy. What the hell is going through your head? I am not that old. Don't you think that Pamela and I look like sisters? Lio: Call her "beautiful mama." She will love you more!

**Greg:** I called the travel agency and made a reservation for two sleeping cars to New York. You, my dear mother-in-law, will come with us. I will sleep in one car and you and Pamela will sleep in the other.

**Sue:** You are trying to tell me that on the first night of your marriage I will sleep with you wife. This is crazy, it is crazy. What are People going to say when they find out?

**Greg:** Dear Mom, this is necessary. I will reward you for the rest of your life!

**Pamela:** Excuse me, but can I say something? Tell me, Greg, why is this so necessary?

**Sal:** (In a corner of the room in an aside.) This is what I expected. If everything goes according to plan, I will be the winner!

**Lio:** Greg, my dear son-in-law! You know that I do not talk a lot, but I do not think this is a good idea to take your mother-in-law with you unless you have lost your mind!

**Greg:** Listen, Dad, Lio, I will explain everything. Sal has convinced me how to approach the situation and tried to help me. (Greg, Lio, and Sal form a group and discuss the matter.)

**Pamela:** Mother! I do not understand. I really do not understand why Greg is acting this way.

**Sue:** Oh, my beautiful daughter, do not ask me. I am in the dark. I just heard that the telegram that Greg received has changed everything. I will stay close to you every minute. Please do not get scared. I will protect you.

**Pamela:** Mama, thank you. I love you very much. I am so happy that you will be coming with us. I am scared. (Gets close to her mother and hugs her.) I am scared!

**Sue:** Please, baby, do not get scared . . . why are you scared? Your mama will protect you. (Lio interrupts the conversation.)

**Lio:** (To his wife.) Let's go, Sue, you are late. Go fix your suitcase. If you want to go to New York and catch the flight to Paris, then you better hurry. The case is in your favor, go . . . go . . . and hurry.

**Sue:** Me! Go to New York? Fly to Paris.

**Lio:** Do not take too long. We do not have lots of time at our disposal. Please do not forget anything. I'll go look for the passport. If I can remember, they are in my desk. (Lio and Sue exit from the scene.)

**Greg:** (Gets close to Pamela and hugs her very tightly.) Do not worry, my beautiful wife. You will be with me for the rest of your life. We will have lots of time, just you and I.

> (Lio enters the room; he has the passport to his wife and another to his daughter.)

Pamela and Sue, open the passport to check that everything is in order!

**Sue:** Oh, God! Do you see the date? This passport expired last month. Oh, God, nothing's going right. Lio, what are we going to do? Please, Pamela, look at yours. I bet yours is expired too. If I remember the last time, we used these was on our last vacation we had together.

**Pamela:** Oh . . . Mama, you're right . . . mine is expired too . . . please do not tell me that I can't go with Greg . . . . Please do not tell me that!

> (Sue gets close to console her daughter.)

**Greg:** Please, do not get dramatic. Everything will be fine. It will just take a few days to stamp your passports. I will change the date for your reservation and you can catch up with me . . . .

**Pamela:** You would leave without me? (Talking to Greg.)

**Greg:** Tell me, my love, what am I supposed to do? You know that it is necessary that I go.

**Sal:** (To Greg.) I know that you bought the tickets. If you like I will come with you. My passport is always in order.

**Lio:** My passport is in order too. (Turns to Sue.) Please do not think that I would like to leave you alone, but Greg has to leave. I do not mind going to New York. In the meantime, you and Pamela get the passports stamped and catch up with us. (To Sal.) It would be nice if you come with us. Your presence would be useful. Greg would be happy and I do not like to be alone.

    (Greg, Pamela, and Sue form a circle. Sal leaves his place where the gifts are.)

**Sue:** (To Lio.) You are magic. You resolved everything in your own way.

**Pamela:** No! I do not want Greg going without me………. No!

**Lio:** Please calm down! Everything will be okay. Come on, we still have some guests to be welcomed. We have to be together, let's go ....

**Pamela:** Please! You go. I will not show my face in this condition. I am a mess. I'll see them later!

**Lio:** Oh, God! What a day! I have to do everything, everything! Let's Go, Greg.

    (Greg kisses his wife and goes out with Lio.)

**Sue:** (Going out of the scene.) What a day, what a day … too many things on my mind.

(Frances enters.)

**Frances:** Oh, Pamela! My dear Pamela, my friend … you are the most beautiful bride I have ever seen, let me hug you. (She whispers something in Pamela's ear.) When you get back from the honeymoon, promise me that you will tell me everything with all the details. You promise?

**Pamela:** I promise! My friend, I promise I will tell you every detail. I won't leave anything out.

**Frances:** Please do not be like all my other friends who got married. They said they would tell me everything about the honeymoon, but then they changed their mind. I do not understand why!

**Pamela:** No, my dear friend. I promise I will tell you everything.

**Frances:** Now, I have to go! Let me hug you one more time ……… Let me kiss you. I hope you have the best honeymoon ever …. good-bye. I'll see you when you both get back. Have a good trip!

(To Sal who enters.) Hi, Sal, good luck! (She exits.)

**Sal:** Good luck! (He looks around.) Good luck for what?

**Attorney Conti:** (Enters to accompany Lio.) (To Pamela.) Good luck! Good luck for a new married life.

**Pamela:** Thank you. Thank you very much, Attorney Conti. And Mrs. Conti, how is she doing?

**Attorney Conti:** She is doing fine. She is in the other room talking with some friends.

**Pamela:** I have to excuse myself, I have to say hello to Mrs. Conti. Excuse me. (Exits.)

**Attorney Conti:** (Sal gets close.) My dear Sal, how are you doing?

**Sal:** Hi, Attorney Conti. Everything is fine. It has been a long time since we have seen each other.

**Attorney Conti:** Yes . . . it has been a couple of months, but I've been keeping my ears open. I have heard a lot of things about you.

**Watch** out, you can't get caught in the net. Listen to my advice. I will talk to you some other time. I have to go see my wife in the other room. If she does not see me for ten minutes, she gets worried. Lio, all me, let me know when you will be a grandfather. I hope it is soon.

**Lio:** Please, my friend, just the word "grandfather" makes me sound like an old man. I am still too young to be a grandfather. Good-bye, my friend. Thank you for coming.

(The attorney exits.)

**Sal:** (Loudly.) Good-bye, Attorney Conti!

**Sal:** (To Sal.) Bye, I'll see you. I have to go see what's going on. We have to leave for the train in a few minutes.

(Lio leaves the stage.)

**Sal:** (Ready to leave.)

**Teresa:** (Enters.) Where are we going?

**Sal:** To Paris. Now I have to go home. I have to change my suit and then I'll be ready. My dear friend, I have to go far away from you. I hear lots of gossip around. Everybody thinks that you and I have something going on. I have to go because I promised myself that Pamela will pay for the way she treats me. She left me for Greg and the only thing he can do is kick a ball.

**Teresa:** But Greg is a gentleman. He never did anything wrong to anyone.

**Sal:** I do not understand. You never change, you always like what I detest. I do not know why, but don't you think if we had something in common, we would get along very well.

**Teresa:** Let's have some serious talk. In reality I think you have to be self-assured. Love that comes at first sight does not last forever. It is only infatuation before two people fall in love seriously. You need to get married, you have to have a kid, you have to live together and then maybe you can talk about love.

**Sal:** I do not think the same way you do. For me love is love at first sight. The first look tells me everything. Blind love is more passionate. It's full of adventure.

**Teresa:** Blind love! Do you know what the hell are you saying? Don't you know that as time passes by the reality will surface? All the faults, the tormented life of the past will surface. The bad habits that you thought were merit will transmit into hate; no passion will be there. Everything will cease to exist. Who will pay the consequences?

**Sal:** You are trying to tell me that the people who know each other will have a better future! Do not make me laugh. Tell me how they would have a better future. Tell me you have experience. You can be honest with me.

**Teresa:** No! I do not want to say that everything will be hate. But think more seriously what will happen, your friendship, the disappointment, the desire. Things that two people have in common sometime diverge, and then what happens? I'll tell you what happens? (Sal interrupts Teresa.)

**Sal:** You want to say that honesty and a yes in front of a priest will give you a tranquil way to a long relationship. I say very dull. . . .

**Teresa:** Your way of thinking is very different from mine. You think that a big account at the bank will do everything that you want, or make you have the luxury of having all the women that you want for a one-stand. And then the next day they go around and tell their friends that adventure of the night before and have some good laughs at the stupid man who spent money for hours of a good time. Maybe just a caress or a kiss without making love can cost them a bounty of money.

**Sal:** What are you trying to say?

**Teresa:** I'm trying to say you have a to get through your thick head that you have to stop living the way that you do. Don't you get tired of buying love? Wouldn't you like to find a nice woman whom you could spend for the rest of your life with. To go home to at night and tell her beautiful words, caress her, give her all your love, be a father, and have a baby call your name who would play with you, have a family. . . . I would give everything to be a mother, to be called mom, to give my love to a man of my life.

**Sal:** I've never heard you talk like that. You are sincere. I am touched and I appreciate you words full of tenderness, but how long will this last? Maybe I am mistaken, maybe I am crazy. I have no time now! I have decided to go to Paris! Good-bye.

ACT TWO

**Scene:** A big room that looks like a restaurant, and is divided into three sections. Each of the sections has a different name that is written on top. The first section is called séparé Rouge . . . the second section is called séparé Le Blanc . . . the third is called séparé Daisy . . . From the séparé Le Blanc, a bell (like a church bell) ring. Rachael, the starlet at the café, enters.

**Rachael:** Waiter!!! Waiter!!!

**Waiter:** (Runs onto the stage.) Sorry, Miss Rachael, sorry. I am so Busy tonight that I wish I took the day off!!! The soccer team from the U.S.A. is going to have a party and everything has got to be perfect. What can I do for you?

**Rachael:** I do not really care who you are waiting for. I am tired of calling you so many times. The service tonight is so bad that I would leave if I weren't waiting for an important man. Let me ask you, this is the right séparé that is reserved for me?

**Waiter:** Yes, Lady Rachael, this is the right séparé reserved just for you. If you like I can go check with the manager . . . would you like another martini or something else?

**Rachael:** Thank you!!! Thank you!!! If you do not mind, I would like some information about the gentleman I have been waiting for. I understand that you know him.

**Waiter:** I am very sorry, my dear Miss Rachael, but I do not know this gentleman very well. I can tell you he is very elegant; it is very distinct, and a ladylike man. He is also a very generous tipper. I wish everybody would be like him. My eyes can tell when somebody is a gentleman or not and I do not make mistakes very easily. Look, he's coming. (Sal walks onto the stage.) Call me when you need me.

   (Waiter leaves the stage.)

**Sal:** Miss Rachael? I am so sorry to let you wait, but it took me so much longer than I had expected and I am sorry for that!!! Would you like to have something to drink? I'll have a martini.

(Rings the bell. The waiter comes.)

**Waiter:** What can I do for you, sir?

**Sal:** Two martinis, please, with olives, thank you. (The waiter leaves.) Tell me, Miss Rachael, as in everything.

**Rachael:** You are a lucky man because another two minutes of waiting and I would have left. What kept me waiting was the curiosity to see you in person, see your elegant way of doing things.

**Waiter:** (Brings two martinis to the table.) Excuse me, please . . . thank you. Anything else you need, just ring the bell. (Leaves.)

**Rachael:** What did your note say last night? I do not recall. I had too many martinis, but you did the right thing to put that piece of paper into my pocketbook. Otherwise, I would not be here. Now if you like, you have to start all over again because I remember nothing.

**Sal:** Do not worry. It is nothing special to remember. It is an easy service with plenty of money to make. I think you are going to like it very much. Do you know that in the other room the American soccer team is having dinner? In a while you will call the waiter and you will give him this note. It is an invitation and you will tell the waiter to give the note to the soccer player named Greg Pite. I do not think that this is very a hard way to make money? (Sal gives the note to Rachael.)

**Rachael:** (She gets the note and she reads.) That's what I have to do? Just that? I have to make sure that the soccer player from the U.S.A. team gets this note? For me that is an honor!!!

**Sal:** Yes! I told you it would be a simple task. Eventually you will enjoy his company. I am sure of that.

**Rachael:** (Reads the note again in a loud voice.) I will wait for you at the Le Blanc séparé, please do not disappoint me. I watched the game and I am very interested to have your acquaintance to congratulate you in person. My happiness and euphoria goes to

**all** of the players, but especially to you. That second goal you scored made you so insuperable, I was so excited that I threw my hat into the air and I never found it. Please let me meet you.

**Sal:** Do not worry about the hat. I will buy you dozens of hats if you like, but tell me, is this a good way to introduce yourself?

**Rachael:** Thank you for your offer. You are so generous to obtain something that interests you!!! But do not worry, I will make sure that what you ask me to do will be done with art and passion. I am sure that the champ will fall into my arms like a baby, and when he is next to me, he will forget everything and everyone.

**Sal:** I like the way you talk. I just love you, really. And do not worry, I will take care of you and much more. . . .

**Rachael:** Very generous!! Let me see what is going to happen. I will make my best effort to make him happy. You know that I can convince any man to do what I want. This is my job, and believe me, I have a lot of experience.

**Sal:** Listen, Rachael, what is your real name? You know that I go to all the shows, but I do not remember ever reading your name in any of the manifestos. Maybe I do not pay any attention, but tell me if you use a stage name. (Teresa starts to come in. She sees Rachael and Sal talking and stays behind and listens to everything.)

**Rachael:** Listen! You should know that no star in this world uses her real name. The retention of private life is more important than any show. My name here in France is Belnome, so that it looks more Italian and remember that French people adore the Italian star, and producer looks for Italian!!!

**Sal:** I understand. Well, where are we . . . oh . . . after you give the note to the waiter and the champ comes to meet you, please try to be very pleasant. Use your personality. Be sexy and show him everything you've got!!!

**Rachael:** Please!!! You do not expect me to be naked by any chance?

**Sal:** I never thought that you would go so far into detail, but if you

**like,** I will never stop you. It is important that you accomplish what we are here for.

**Rachael:** Sal! You have to have faith. You have to trust me if you want everything to go the way you planned. I'll tell you that my body is capable of doing everything and having the best result. Remember that my first job I got was because of the way I move the hours I spend at the gym gives me the result. Trust me, you will get what you have asked for.

**Sal:** You are an altruist. I know that and I like it because you show your class in a womanly way to obtain what you want.

**Rachael:** Don't worry. That superstar will fall like a fish falls in to a net.

**Sal:** Oh . . . Rachael, your voice makes my body tremble, my blood boil. But for now, we are here for business. I hope that later you will give me ten minutes of your time. You are stupendous.

**Rachael:** With your compliments you make me feel sexier than I am, but you know for the right price, I would give you ten  minutes of my time. I know that money is not an object for you, but we will have to postpone this intimate encounter that I am sure will last longer than ten minutes. I have to go now. I have to be ready and beautiful for the superstar. . . .

**Sal:** Come here, Rachael! Before you start this new adventure, come close, sit on my lap. You are very attractive lady. I start to get jealous thinking about somebody else getting to touch your body before me.

    (Sal hugs Rachael and kisses her. Teresa sees everything from behind the door where she observed that long discussion.)

**Rachael:** (After the kiss, recomposes herself.) I have to tell you, sometimes you can be a gentleman. A really neat man to be with. Maybe after we conclude this business with the soccer player, we can get together for a few hours of passion. Not just for money but for the way you handle my body. Now you have to excuse me. I have to go before I commit another sin. We must postpone this discussion for later.

    (She leaves the stage.)

**Sal:** (He composes himself.) Ah . . . it's you!!! Only you can do that, follow me all over the world. Would you like to tell me what the  hell you are doing in Paris? I know you like to drive me crazy. You want to make me insane with your presence in every corner of the world.

**Teresa:** Oh . . . Sal! My dear Sal, always impeccable! Really impeccable. Nobody in this world can do it like you, always busy with beautiful girls!!! So busy that you forgot to ask how I am doing or just to say hi . . .

**Sal:** Hi, Teresa, my dear Teresa!!! I am so happy to see you again any place that I go!!! You in Paris!!! I can see you are very relaxed. I hope you rested after the long trip. I wouldn't mind if you entertained me for a while. You follow me all over, you travel thousands of miles just to spy on me. At Greg and Pamela's wedding, you did not leave me for a moment even when I tried to get away from you. You and your mentality make everybody believe that you and I have something going on. People think that you are my fiancée. I think that this is too much to take. This is one of the reasons that I came to Paris. I do not know why you took the next plane and followed me and I do not know anymore how to get rid of you.

**Teresa:** Please! Calm, calm. . . . I did not take the next plane, I waited till the next day so people wouldn't think I was following you!!!

**Sal:** I am calm . . . very calm . . . I am trying very hard not to lose my patience, but I see by your sarcasm you are trying to exasperate me!!!

**Teresa:** I personally think that your interpretation of my actions is completely different from mine. I really like you and I am concerned about you. I do not want anything to happen to you.

(She gets very close to him.)

Please try to use your imagination. Don't you see that my body wants yours?

**Sal:** Please, not here!!! Do not tell me that you came to Paris just to Offer me your body!

**Teresa:** I am here to keep an eye on you and to suggest that it is not the right thing to do to get cheap sex because someday you will regret it!

**Sal:** Thank you . . . thank you very much for your concern, but I think that it is not necessary that you are so thoughtful about me. I am old enough to control my sex drive.

**Teresa:** But wait, do not think that I came to Paris just for you. Remember that I have a lot of friends here. They call me in America to invite me to come and vacation here in Paris. To be honest with you, I came to keep my eyes open. I do not want anything to happen to Pamela. I will protect her. She belongs to her husband and nobody else. I hope you understand me!!!

**Sal:** This explanation and affection that you have for Pamela really touches me inside. For now, I understand that you are my adversary and I hope you will stay that way for a long time.

**Teresa:** On the contrary, don't misunderstand. The friendship that we have, the remembrance of the time that we spent together. I would like to avoid you, to not let you feel embarrassed towards me.

**Sal:** I understand!!!! You do not want to give me that foolishness in front of other people.

**Teresa:** Not like you say, but you're starting to make your brain work more than you usually do. If you acknowledged all of the faults that you have, then you are in the right direction and this is what I want. (Pamela and her mother are entering.)

**Sue:** Sal!! Teresa!!! What a beautiful place!!! I would have expected more exposition of antique art. These walls are empty. I personally do not think that this is such a classy place. What do you think my dear Teresa? (Sal gets in the middle of the discussion.)

**Sal:** Maybe this was the only one available in the short period of time when the team made it to the finals. Do not worry, you will see that this place will transform. I will make sure of that!!! I am sure you will like it, especially at night when all of the high-class people fill up every corner of this place. Don't forget, my dear Sue, you are in Paris, the city with a thousand faces. (To Pamela.) Alone here!!! Where is your faithful husband?

**Teresa:** Listen, Pamela, don't pay attention!!! Sal, you are a . . . you knew that Greg couldn't be with us right now. He had to go be with the press. All of the interviews will keep him away for a while. Please don't be so stupid. Greg will be here, just be patient. He will be here!!!

**Sue:** (To Teresa.) Did you see the game? Please tell me all the details. Sal can't tell me anything!!!

**Sal:** Excuse me!!! Do you forget that when the team was playing, I was at the airport waiting for you? Maybe you forgot that the plane was three hours late. Please don't be so arrogant!!!

**Sue:** I apologize. Sal is right. The trip was a disaster. We left late from New York and the weather was so bad, but I thank God that we are here in one piece.

**Sal:** I stay and wait for over five hours . . . do you realize how many times I went to the information window and asked about why the plane was late?

**Sue:** Thank you, my dear friend!!! But do not tell me you were irritated because the plane was late!!!

**Pamela:** (To Teresa.) I am sure that you saw the game. You can not imagine my disappointment not to be there and cheer my husband along for the excellent game that he played and carried the team to victory.

**Teresa:** What I can't say you will see in the newspaper tomorrow. Greg was the best player on the field. It was extraordinarily good and I heard that if he weren't there, the team would have lost. The winning goal was his merit.

**Sal:** Like a racehorse, he was in good form!!!

**Sue:** Our Greg, I am so proud to hear such words. I am so proud that he is my daughter's husband. He is a good man and I am sure that he will make Pamela very happy. He has natural skills and will be a famous player. Teresa, if you do not mind, I would like to look around for a while. Pamela, are you coming with us?

**Teresa:** Oh, yes. I have a lot to show you like I promised. (Sue and Pamela follow Teresa on the way out.)

**Sal:** Please, Pamela. I would like it if you stayed here. I have to talk to you!

**Pamela:** You want to talk to me? About what . . . didn't you hear we are ready to go out?

**Sal:** Pamela, please!!! Don't you act like that. Who was at this airport when you arrived waiting there for you? Who was the first one to make you feel welcome in Paris? Please tell me . . . now I just asked you to stay here because I would like to talk to you and you refuse to talk to me?

**Pamela:** (Toward her mother and Teresa.) Please, Mom, go with Teresa and I will see you later. (Teresa and Sue leave the stage.) Sal, why did you do that to me? Why do you want me to feel sorry for you? Whatever you do for me and my family is because you are a good friend, and believe me, we will never forget that.

**Sal:** Excuse me. I know that all of you will never forget me, but tell me, dear Pamela, why me?

**Pamela:** If I am correct, you came here to Paris because my father asked you to.

**Sal:** This is what everybody thinks, but the reality is that I am here because of you . . . you know the way I feel about you, even if you are married, my body, my soul can't be far away from you. I hope you understand. Even if I don't see you or touch you, you make me feel like I am part of you. . . .

**Pamela:** But you have to realize that I love Greg, that Greg is my husband, and I will never be unfaithful to him because I love him very much.

**Sal:** Pamela … oh, Pamela, you can still save yourself from this miserable relationship. You are so candid. You do not realize what you have gotten into. Your husband is a superstar, he will never have time to spend with you. You can tell he is a very busy man. Since you arrived in Paris, you have not heard a word from him. Tell me what husband would do something like that. Listen, the temptation this city is so strong. I just hope that your husband does not fall in the trap very easily.

**Pamela:** I know that you are jealous, but I can trust Greg with my life. He would never be unfaithful to me. He loves me, he doesn't care about any other women, and remember that he never consummated our first night of marriage.

**Sal:** Please tell me what you would do if you found out that Greg was unfaithful to you?

**Pamela:** No!!! You want me to believe that Greg is staying away from me with the excuse of having an interview. This is impossible. I can't believe that. . . .

**Sal:** Greg is sure of himself. He knew in his mind that after the wedding you couldn't get rid of him. Remember that a marriage is a contract that keeps two people tied. This is a personal certainty for a woman, and for a man, it is so nothing happens to the relationship. For now, Greg enjoys his freedom!!!

**Pamela:** Please, Sal, don't be so stupid!!! I trust Greg, I trust him with my life . . .

(The waiter passes by to serve a drink.)

**Sal:** I am a man. I have an instinct that before Greg consummates his first night of marriage, he has no other choice but to be in another woman's arms. I can bet on that!!! If you don't believe me, I will make sure you will see it with your own eyes, but you to promise that you won't get mad at me. When this happens, you have to be very strong in your decision. I personally don't believe that any man should betray his woman before consummating his marriage.

**Pamela:** (With an unpleasant tone of voice.) Please stop. I can't take your accusations any longer. You are starting to make me mad. Don't you see that you are not making any sense? If you don't stop right now, I will lose what little respect I have for you. I don't believe a word that you have said. Please, I don't want to hear anymore!!!

**Sal:** I am trying my best to let you see the reality of things.

(Lio, Sue, and Teresa enter.)

**Pamela:** (Walks toward her mother.) Mother, please help me. I do not know what to think. I believe Sal is right that Greg should have never left me the day of our wedding, but I'm trying very hard to not make a big issue out of it. This period of my life is very difficult.

**Sue:** My dear Pamela, I do understand and I don't want you to think that I am taking Greg's side, but I believe that he had no other choice but to go to Paris with the soccer team. This is his future and to be correct, yours too. He is your husband and whatever he is going to accomplish in life is not just for him but for the future of his family. I think that in this moment he is thinking about the way you think about him. He loves you and I am sure of that and when this is all over and we go back to America, you will be the happiest wife in the world.

**Lio:** Please, not now. Let's try to stay calm and you, Sal, please try to stop instigating the situation. I am sure that everything will be okay after all this is over and we go back home. (To Sal.) Please keep the women company. As you all know, I have the honor of being invited to the ceremony. I would love to stay with you all, but it was impossible for me to refuse.

(From the other hall, some noise is heard.)

**You** all have dinner in the dining room and I and Greg will join you after the banquet, and please join Sal's dinner without arguing.

**Sal:** Don't worry!!! I am sure that everything will be okay and these beautiful women will enjoy my company.

(Sue, Teresa, and  Pamela looks at each other with grimaces.)

We will have our own séparé far away from the crowd.

**Teresa:** I do not understand why we have to eat by ourselves. I think that if we eat with all the other people, it would be more pleasant.

**Lio:** I am sorry but I insist, I think that if you all eat with all of the other guests it wouldn't look good. We are different, we have more class.

**Teresa:** I think you are right. It is better if we eat in our séparé. We can still have a good time.

**Sue:** I think Lio is right for the first time in his life!!!

**Sal:** I will inform the waiter. (Greg enters.)

**Pamela:** Greg!!! Oh, my love. (She runs to hug and kiss him.) You cannot imagine the unhappiness that I have in me because you have not been here with me. I know that I should be the happiest woman in the world, but I want you to be with me. I don't want to spend one more hour far away from you.

**Greg:** My dear Pamela, you know that I adore you, that I love you more than my life. I will not be away from you for long. I promise that after the toast I will be here with you and never leave you alone again.

**Sal:** Paris … Paris … what a city, sometime makes the reality vanish. Love has got to be strong; nobody can tell what is going to happen in this city of lechery.

**Pamela:** (To Greg.) I would like to go far away from here, far away, just you and me, to be by ourselves far away from this torment, from this air that smells pollution. I want to be with you in a meadow and smell the perfume of the flowers, make love under the sky full of stars. Forget this city, forget the soccer team that took you away from me on the day of our wedding.

**Greg:** Yes, my love, my desire is to have you just for me far away from everybody. Just you and I breathing love words that only you can feel and touching your velvet skin under the stars … but please have a little more patience. I will be back and we will fulfill our dream. (To Lio.) Let's go, my dear father-in-law, we have this last formal banquet to attend. (Toward Pamela and others.) You all try to have a good time, get whatever you want. The team will pick up the tab. I'll see you very soon!!!

**Pamela:** You're leaving so soon!!! We just got to see each other for a minute and now you're leaving!!!

**Greg:** My love! (Gets close and kisses her.) Please, my love, don't make me feel guilty. You know that I have to attend this banquet for the team. I told you I will be back soon. I can't wait till this is over. I am tired of all these people and interviewing. Please have a little more patience!!!

**Sal:** I told you! Paris is contagious! Can change anybody. Maybe it's the air, but it looks like he is changing to me.

**Pamela:** (To Greg.) Please tell me!!! By any chance with all of this publicity, did you find someone better looking than me?

**Greg:** Please!!! Stop!!! Don't say stupid things. I love you and only you, and no one is more beautiful than you. You are my wife.

**Pamela:** Please don't leave me. Renounce all of this formality. The banquet is not necessary. I implore you; you can sacrifice all of this for me because I am your wife.

**Greg:** You know that I can't renounce the banquet. Everybody will be there. What am I going to tell the technical director when he does not see me? I promise that I won't stay a minute longer than is necessary.

**Lio:** Greg, let's go. We are late and they are looking for you right now.

**Greg:** (To Pamela.) I'll see you soon, my love, and we will be together forever.

**Sal:** I hope for a better future!!! My dear Pamela, with a husband like yours, you've got to have a lot of patience.

**Sue:** What are you trying to insinuate?

**Pamela:** I am here just for him and he leaves me. I think that he doesn't understand my suffering and desire to be his wife!!!

**Sue:** Please, Pamela, stay calm. (To Greg.) Greg, I trust you. After the banquet no excuses. You have to come back here with us. You too, Lio. Do not forget we will be expecting you. You know that I get mad very easily!!! Get out of here and hurry!!! Let's go eat. Our séparé should be ready. I am hungry. (They all leave the stage very slowly.)

**Lio:** Yes, my love. Don't worry, we will be back as soon as it is over. (Sal and Lio exit.)

**(Rachael** followed by the waiter, enters the stage.)

**Waiter:** Miss Rachael, the séparé that I reserved for you is ready.

**Rachael:** Thank you very much. Please don't forget that when the banquet is over, I would like to meet this famous player. I want to congratulate him personally for the victory of the team.

**Waiter:** Don't worry, Miss Rachael. Greg will be here. He has some relatives waiting in the other séparé.

**Rachael:** If he has some other woman waiting for him, I think she will not have a chance. I will meet him before he goes to the other séparé. I adore athletes who become well known, and it is my style to give them the best that I've got.

**Waiter:** I know the way you do it, but this time I think you are too late. I don't think the name Mr. Pite will be written in your diary. In the other séparé, someone is waiting for him. A very beautiful lady. She gave me a note to give to Mr. Pite when I serve him at the banquet.

**Rachael:** I ask you, do not give that note to anyone!!!

**Waiter:** You know that I can't do that. The lady that gave it to me said she would take care of me very well, and it is my duty as you know to be professional at my job. You know that I am and people respect me for that.

**Rachael:** And I will take care of you better, but you have to promise me that Mr. Pite never gets the note. You understand that!!!

**Waiter:** Miss Rachael! People who come here know me very well and they know that I am very conscientious when I have to follow instructions, but I also say that anyone can make a mistake, especially with all of these people who are here right now. I notice that close to Mr. Pite is one of his family members. I can give the note to him and say I made a mistake. This can happen if you are really generous.

**Rachael:** I like you more and more. I like the way you think. You will not be sorry for this favor. Just keep an eye on him. I want him to get out from this side!!!

**Waiter:** I will keep an eye on Mr. Pite and I will make sure that he comes out from this side, like you requested. This just for you because you are so generous and I will never forget that. (He bows and starts to leave the stage.)

**Rachael:** (Laughs at him in a special way, then gets some money out of her purse and gives it to him. She leaves the stage.)

**Teresa:** (Enters the stage and calls the waiter.) Waiter . . . waiter!!!

**Waiter:** (Talking to himself.) I hope this is not another woman looking for the soccer player. Yes!!! Miss, you called me? What can I do for you?

**Teresa:** Please, I would like to know if inside the séparé is a young woman. Her name is Rachael!!!

**Waiter:** I am so sorry, my dear lady, but I can't tell the name of the lady in the séparé. It is very private, and confidentiality in this place is important.

**Teresa:** (Opens her purse.) Take this, this is for you. (She offers money to the waiter.) Listen, I know that you have a note to give to give to Greg, sorry, Mr. Pite, soccer player. I just want to know the contents. I hope I'm not asking too much!!!

**Waiter:** Listen, I told you that my position in my job prevents my seeing the contents of the note.

**Teresa:** (Opens her purse again and gives more money to the waiter.) Take this, this is yours. (The waiter takes the note from his pack and lets it drop to the floor. Teresa picks up the note, reads it very fast, and gives it back to the waiter.) Thank you!!!

**Waiter:** You are a very lucky lady. Fortunately, you convinced me; otherwise, you would have never known the contents of the note.

**Teresa:** I beg you, please do not give the note to Greg, sorry, Mr. Pite. That note has to disappear. It is very important. You do not understand the importance of why that note mustn't be delivered!!!

**Waiter:** (Very quickly puts the note in his pack.) I am very sorry for whatever reason, but I have to deliver that note. You know that I have to do my job. People depend on me for all the dirty jobs!!! (Teresa gets more money and gives it to the waiter.) In that case, my beautiful lady, I can make a little mistake and maybe I can give the note to someone sitting next to this famous player Greg or Mr. Pite and say that I made a mistake. I hope someday you will appreciate what I did for you.

**Teresa:** I do not know how to thank you. Thank you, thank you again!!!

**Waiter:** You do not have to thank me. It is my duty to satisfy my clientele. (Exits.)

**Sal:** (Comes in the stage a little angry as he sees Teresa.) You still here? What are you doing here?

**Teresa:** Slow down, my dear friend, slow down. Why do you ask me with that tone of voice?

**Sal:** I don't understand!!! I do not understand!!!

**Teresa:** You always pretend not to understand when something happens. You never change, never.

**Sal:** No! This time I am not kidding. I am very serious. I do not understand!!!

**Teresa:** I do not know what happened to you. Sometimes you are very arrogant. I do not know what I did to you to be treated like this!!! Why are you trying to avoid me? Why?

**Sal:** No! This is not right that you say that. You know that every time

> I see you it is a pleasure. Right now, is not the right time. I have no rancor against you. You take advantage of the interest that I have in you.

**Teresa:** Rancor!!! Rancor for what? Because I am here in Paris too? You know that I have a lot of friends here and every year they want me to come here on a vacation. I should be mad the way you are treating me. I think you should apologize and be more of a gentleman!!!

**Sal:** We are too close friends to stay apart and fight, but if you want me to apologize for my behavior, I will. Please accept my apology!!!

**Teresa:** You are trying to tell me that from now on you will be a gentleman towards me just because we are friends!!!

**Sal:** No. I do not want to say that. I just want to say that we are friends, good friends!

**Teresa:** In that case if you apologize and you are my friend, then let's shake hands.

**Sal:** With pleasure. (He shakes hands with Teresa.) Excuse me. (He looks at his watch.) Do not forget we have to go to meet the others . . . .

**Teresa:** I know . . . I know . . . .

**Sal:** Please you go . . . I will follow you in a few minutes.

**Teresa:** I'm going. I will see you in a few minutes. (She starts to leave when unexpectedly she starts to faint. She holds herself on a chair.) Sal!!! Please, Sal, I am not feeling well. I fainted, my head, my head is spinning and I do not know why. Please help me!!!

**Sal:** (With disappointment.) This is the right time for her to faint. What an excuse!!!

**Teresa:** (Holds on to Sal) Thank you, thank you. You have to excuse me. I do not know what happened. My head just started to spin. I will be okay. I do not know what I would have done if you were not here. Thank you. (Helps Teresa sits on the chair.) In a few minutes, I will feel better. Please if you do not mind take me on the other side. I think my legs are still shaking, but in a while, I will be fine. . . .

**Sal:** Do not worry. I am here, I will hold you, let's go. (They exit.)

(A bell rings and Rachael appears on the front of her séparé with a dress so transparent it shows her body in full form.)

**Rachael:** (To the waiter who came on the stage after hearing the bell ring.) Did you deliver my note? If you did not deliver it yet, please try to do so because I am starting to get annoyed. I never would have imagined that I would have to wait all this time. If I knew, I never would have accepted to meet this famous player. I have better things to do with my time. (She gets back in her séparé and waits.)

**Sal:** (Walks on stage.) Waiter!!! Waiter!!! I am going to be in the other séparé. When you see Greg and Rachael talking, please just come to see me, but do not say a word. I will understand. I just want to notice you.........

(Exits.)

**Waiter:** Do not worry. I will do the way you say so to. I will go right now and give him the note.

**Rachael:** (Looks through the séparé.) I hear some noise. Maybe the banquet is over. I hear someone walking, coming this way. (She gets into the séparé.)

**Waiter:** (Lio, followed by the waiter, enters.) Excuse me, sir!!! I have a note for you!!!

**Lio:** A note for me? And who gave you this note?

**Waiter:** Sorry, sir, this is very confidential. I can't reveal the person who gave me the note. I'll just tell you that it is one of the most beautiful women you have ever seen in this place. She told me to give it personally to you.

**Lio:** She is young; she is beautiful. Are you sure that this note is for me?

**Waiter:** Yes, it is for you and you will not be sorry to meet this woman. She is incomparable to any other woman you have ever known. (Sue sees her husband talking with the waiter.)

**Lio:** (Gets the note and reads.) I think I will take a chance. It is a long time since I met another woman. . . .

**Waiter:** I'll tell you, she is like a flower, believe me. (Lio gives a tip to the waiter.) Please sir, this way. (He shows the séparé where Rachael is waiting.)

**Lio:** (Enters the séparé. Sue observes this.)

**Sue:** My husband in a separe? With whom? I do not understand. Maybe I do not see very well. He's betraying me with another woman. I do not believe it, I have to find out. . . . (She retires.)

**Waiter:** (Goes to Rachael séparé.) Miss Rachael, the banquet is over. I told Mr. Pite that someone very special wanted to meet him for a few minutes. He knows where you are; you can't miss him. You will notice him when approaches your séparé. (Leaves.)

**Greg:** (Enters.) Who is this person who wants to meet me? I do not see anyone, I can't be left alone. . . .

**Rachael:** (She was looking from her séparé. As soon as she sees Greg, she comes out and throws herself into Greg's arms.) You are Mr. Pite, Greg. Yes, sorry. Greg, I am so confused you are the champ, you are sexy. I just want to congratulate you for the superlative game that you played. (She does not give Greg time to react and kisses him with passion. Right in that moment, Pamela, Sal, Teresa, and Sue enter. As soon as Pamela sees the Scene, she screams and comes out from Rachael's séparé.

**Rachael** follows Lio half naked, then gets back into her séparé.)

**Sue:** (To her husband.) You will pay for that, you will pay. For now, let me take care of my daughter. (She kneels on the floor.) Pamela, Pamela, my baby, wake up. Are you okay? Please give me some water. (To Greg.) You too will pay for that. For now, don't stand there like a pole, help me . . . . You men are all the same. You are only good for one thing and one thing only!!!

**Sal:** I do not understand anything anymore!!! Teresa: What a job you did!!! (To Sal.)

**Greg:** (He kneels by Pamela who opens her eyes.) Oh, my love, my dear love. I love you so much. I am so sorry to cause this to you. Please forgive me. I swear it is not my fault for what has happened. I am so sorry; please forgive me!!!

**Pamela:** (She comes to her senses.) Please go away!!! Don't touch me!!! Go away!!! I don't want to see you!!!

**Sue:** (To her husband.) And you, what an excuse you've got!!! By any chance have you gotten tired of me? Maybe I do not give you enough sex anymore and you need to see another woman to satisfy your manhood. What an excuse you've got!!! When we get home, if I do not divorce you, I will put a chain to your neck so you can't even go to the bathroom without asking my permission. You'll see!!!

**Lio:** I do not understand!!! I really do not understand why this is happening to me!

**Sue:** I heard that Paris was a corrupt city and that women here are so crazy for fame and money they will do anything. (She points at the séparé where Rachael starts to get dressed.) Over there, we've got proof!!!

**Pamela:** I can't believe that I was betrayed by the man whom I love!!! I can't believe this has happened to me. we have not even consummated our first night of marriage and already he has betrayed me. What should I expect of the future when he will leave me for days to go out and play?

**Greg:** (Very sweetly toward Pamela.) Please, Pamela, at least let me explain to you what has happened and then you can be mad at me. But first let me explain. We can leave this matter the way sees it. I don't think I should feel guilty if that girl jumped into my arms and kissed me. I tried. I told her to get off me, but she . . . you see what happens. I love you and I would never change you for another woman for anything in this world. I swear, I swear!!!

**Pamela:** You swear!!! What the hell do you swear? I saw you with my own eyes. You were kissing that b---- and now you swear that you love me!!! What, you want me to see you make love to another woman so you can be sorry again? Please just leave. For now, I don't want to see you, please!!!

**Sal:** I told you not to leave your superstar by himself. I told you that Something would happen; you did not believe me and now!!! I have an idea. Why don't you stay in Paris and get a divorce? It is so simple!!!

**Greg:** Why don't you shut your mouth? You know that I didn't do anything wrong. Maybe you have something to do with all of this scenery. Please, Sal, shut up before I do something that I will regret.

**Lio:** (Toward Sal.) I can't believe that you would say something like that. You know that Greg loves Pamela and he would never do anything to hurt her. I wonder if you have something to do with this. . . . I never want to hear about divorce from your mouth again, do you understand me!!! (Greg tries to keep Pamela calm with the help of Sue. Pamela is upset and cries.)

**Pamela:** Please, I do not want to see anyone right now. I want to be by myself. If all of you want to leave and go back home, then do so!!! Greg, please leave for now. I do not want to see you. Please go home with everybody or with the team. I will see you in Bridgeport. Please go!!!

**Greg:** I can't leave you here in Paris. I am your husband; you have to listen to me. Please, you have to listen. I love you. I can't leave you here.

(He is desperate.)

**Pamela:** (With a sarcastic tone of voice.) I said go away. I don't want to see or speak with you at this moment . . . please

**leave.** . . . I will stay in Paris and if I decide to divorce, I will be considered the divorcée. Please leave, everybody, leave!!!

**Sal:** I told you that this Greg was not the right man!!! (To Pamela.)

I am so sorry.

(Everybody leaves Pamela in the middle of the stage crying.)

57

# ACT THREE

(A few days later in Bridgeport, in the office of Attorney Conti.)

**Scene:** Attorney Conti's office, a few pictures on the wall of an unknown author, two or three diplomas from different universities, a few armchairs, a bookcase, a big table, two doors, one that lets the clientele into the office and the other one connected to his house where he lives with his wife, a desk with a few papers all over the place, a telephone, and a small church bell.

(An old man with a cane enters the office with a young man who is holding him up to make sure he doesn't fall. The young man helps him sit down in a chair next to the table.)

**Attorney:** Please sit down, please!!! Well . . . let's see . . . oh . . . your case!!! Don't you worry; everything is under control. In a few days, I will give you all the information that you need. I am sure that the judge will be on your side!!!

**The Old Man:** Please, Attorney Conti, I trust you!!! You know better than anyone else the way that I care about that property. My family has lived in Bridgeport for more than two hundred years and that property has been passed on from generation to generation, from father to son. I have no doubt that the property is mine. . . . (The phone rings.)

**Attorney:** Excuse me!!! (Picks up the phone.) Oh . . . is you . . . what!!! Even today you take the day off!!! What's a matter with you!!! Don't tell me you are sick again!!! I do not know what to do with you!!! Today I have so many clients to take care of, and in two hours, I have to go to court. Can you please try to come in even for a few hours!!! Good-bye! (Slams the phone.) I do not know what to do. These secretaries are all the same. Nobody wants to work anymore; a little cold and they call in sick, I do not know!!! You need a lot of patience in this world!!!

**The Old Man:** Your secretary is too young to have a responsibility. You know that they like to go out at night and come home very late without thinking that the day after they have to work. Too young!!! I'll give you some advice. Try to get an old secretary and maybe even ugly. You will see that she will never take a day off!!!

**Attorney:** (Looks through a file.) Maybe you are right!!! This is your file. You have nothing to worry about. It is a long process and very expensive, but in the end, you will be satisfied with the result. The judge is in your favor; you will never lose that property. I need your signature here. (Gives some paper to the old man.)

**The Old Man:** (Signs the paper without reading it and gives the paper back to the attorney.) You know that I pray every day to stay in good health. I want to enjoy at least for a few years the property that my parents sweated very hard to acquire. I do not understand how they can take it away from me. The property is mine only mine!!!

**Attorney:** (Trying to organize all the papers on the desk.) I know!!! I know!!!

**The Old Man:** I 'd like to remind you that this case started a long time ago when I was still young. I remember your grandfather when he took the case. Your grandfather, what an attorney he was!!! What a character, a very strong man, he had a voice that intimidated the judge every time he would talk in court.

**Attorney:** Thank you. I know that you are very fond of my family. I will try not to disappoint your expectations. I read the transcript and I see that some of your relatives have tried to take the property from you, but I will make sure that you get everything that is yours.

**The Old Man:** you also have to know that when your grandfather passed away, God bless his soul, your father took over and he tried very hard to help me. Your father, like your grandfather, what an attorney he was. You have to know that when he died this city mourned for a long time. People couldn't believe that he died so young. Sometimes we old people talk about it.

**Attorney:** (Interrupts the old man.) I know that. I was a little boy, but I remember. Maybe I will never be a good attorney like my grandfather or father, but I will make sure that the family tradition of defending people like you will go on for decades to come.

**The Old Man:** I remember that many times the three of us got together and discussed this case for hours with a good glass of wine. Oh . . . what a good time!!!

**Attorney:** I know that it will not be easy, but I am so lucky that my predecessor left everything so organized that I just have to follow the instructions to win this case.

**The Old Man:** I do not know, but I feel very superstitious about this case. I am convinced that when this is all over and finally I will be able to enjoy this piece of land, I will die!!!

**Attorney:** Please don't say things like that. I am sure that you will live another hundred years, but if you really think you will die as soon as this case is over. I will make sure that I will continue your case for a long time.

**The Old Man:** I trust you, young man. Do what you think is right. (He gets up from the chair but starts to fall and the attorney helps him out. They are near to the office door, he starts to exit.) I recommend you, young man, keep your family name high so People don't forget. I salute you. (Exit.)

**Attorney:** I will keep in touch; good-bye for now. (Makes a face.) Oh, God . . . finally, I thought he would never stop talking. I hope this case will be over soon. He is a nice guy, but sometimes!!! (Someone knocks on the door of the office.) Please come in . . .

(An elegant lady comes in.)

**Mrs. Dion:** Good morning, Attorney Conti! I am next in line, so I came in!!!

**Attorney:** Oh . . . I am sorry. Sure, sit down. As you can see, there is paperwork all over. My secretary took the day off, so I have to do everything. Just a few minutes and I will be with you. (Tries to organize some of the papers.) Ok, I think this is enough. I am sorry to let you wait. What can I do for you? Please tell me!!!

**Mrs. Dion:** I am the daughter of Senator Peterson. My husband is John Dion, the Attorney General. I would like to talk to you about something very personal, and if you think it is the right thing to do, I would like you to represent me in this matter.

**Attorney:** It is a pleasure to meet you, Mrs. Dion. I know your family very well and if you'd like to know, your husband and I went to school together. How is he doing? The last time I saw him we were in the Mount. I do not remember the year.

**Mrs. Dion:** I know. He talks about you sometimes. He told me that he knows your family very well, that you two slept in the same room in the Mount to save money!!!

**Attorney:** Oh . . . yes, a long time ago. We stayed at the Den. What a place, very expensive, but very beautiful. We spend a lot of time talking about our young days!!! For me it is an honor to do whatever is in my power to help you even if we do not know each other. For now, you are my friend and whatever I can do, I will not disappoint you.

**Mrs. Dion:** I am pleased that you consider me as a friend because this matter is very intimate and has got to stay such, really confidential between you and me.

**Attorney:** You can talk freely. It's just you and me.

**Mrs. Dion:** Your friend is what this case is about, my husband. I do not know why he betrayed me with another woman. It has been a few months that he has been seeing this woman. I can't take it any longer being treated like this. I would like a separation and maybe a divorce. I would like the court to give me the rights as a wife and I want the truth out in the open. I want a good attorney to represent me.

**Attorney:** But, dear lady, are you sure this is what you want? John is a friend of mine, he is a good man. Maybe he has made a few slips in his life. Are you sure you don't want to reconsider this matter?

**Mrs. Dion:** (Making a face.) Please!!! Attorney Conti Please!!!

**Attorney:** I am sorry!!! If this is what you want. I will try to do my best in keeping my friendship aside and representing you the best way that I know how. Like it or not, divorce is my specialty and my clients are very satisfied for the work that I do for them.

**Mrs. Dion:** Dear Attorney, before I forget I would like to remind you that before I came to see you, I had another attorney and the first time we went to court, the judge denied my plea for a legal separation. Please do not ask who the other attorney was. You are a good friend of his and I am sure that you will find out.

**Attorney:** Dear Lady Dion, we attorneys are not rivals. I am sure that my predecessor tried his best for you. If you tell me who he was, I can talk to him and get some information to prepare my case better for you.

**Mrs. Dion:** I think you know him. It was Attorney Manti, a very honorable man but, I think too old to fight for my rights.

**Attorney:** Attorney Manti!!! Of course, I know him. Peter is a good friend of mine and a good attorney. I personally think one of the best in the field. My dear lady, like I said before, I will try to make you happy in this matter.

**Mrs. Dion:** Attorney Manti could be the best in the world like you say, but when we went to court, I lose my case. You have to do better, you are young, and your ideas are more up-to-date. You know the reason that I came to see you? I think that I deserve some justice. I am still young and if my husband doesn't want me to be his wife, I have to divorce him and try to find the right man for my life!!!

**Attorney:** Oh!!! My dear lady!!! I know that this is a sad situation, but let me say that Attorney Manti is one of the best in the field of divorce cases but just because he was one of my teachers doesn't mean that the student can't be better than the teacher!!! I will represent you and you will be satisfied with the result; you can count on that!!!

**Mrs. Dion:** I have a feeling that you will have no problem. I can see the poison that you have in the way that you talk, and!!! I almost forgot. I found some new documentation that I hope will help you!!!

**Attorney:** What new documentation did you find? Do you have it here? Please let me see!!!

**Mrs. Dion:** They are not really documents, but they can help for sure. I have some pictures that a private photographer took last year at the beach. I was at home like a good wife always is, and my husband, with the excuse of a working trip, went on vacation with his mistress. I had a feeling that he was telling me a lie, so that's when I hired a private investigator to follow my husband, and I was right because when the investigator came back, he showed me the pictures that would tell the truth about my husband's activity with another woman. No more excuses; a picture is worth a thousand words. They tell you everything you want to know!!!

**Attorney:** If you do not mind, I would like to see the pictures. I'll be able to tell you if we can use them in court in your favor, or  not!!!

**Mrs. Dion:** You will see!!! You will see, my dear attorney. I hope that you do not think that I have hired a private investigator just for the fun of it. I did it because I wanted to prove that my husband is unfaithful to me and I do not deserve that.

**Attorney:** Please try to be more specific. We are adults here so you can talk anyway you like. As if we've known each other for a long time, please be more specific. Do not keep any secrets. If you want to win in court, I have to know everything. I hope you understand that. I would like to know what they were doing.

Were they kissing? Were they naked, making love? Please, Mrs. Dion, tell me!!! Please. . . .

**Mrs. Dion:** Kissing!!! Not just kissing, they were in an intimate position. Do you know what I'm trying to tell you? I hope that I do not have to spell it out for you what they were doing!!! But even so, the judge said that was not enough proof to be considered grounds for adultery and to give me a legal separation!!!

**Attorney:** If this is not adultery; I would like to know what is!!! What other proof does the judge want?

**Mrs. Dion:** My husband explained to the judge that that day the water of the sea was agitated and the boat that they were in almost tipped over, but he never told the judge how the woman whom he was with was naked. He said that he tried to save the woman from falling in the water!!! What an excuse!!!

**Attorney:** I hope that we can present other proof, anything that you know can help our case. I think that we have enough evidence, but every little thing will help!!! I do not want to renounce your representation just because the judge is friends with your husband.

**Mrs. Dion:** Please!!! You are my attorney. Try to help me out in this matter. Do not mention that you won't represent me. I will spend all the money that I have to. I just want justice and I don't think that it is the right thing to do, my husband betraying me, just because he is well known. Justice should be equal for everyone!!!

**Attorney:** I will study your case intensely. I can't promise anything, but I will do my best when we get to court.

**Mrs. Dion:** I trust you. I know that everything you will do in court will be in my favor and justice will prevail.

**Attorney:** I wish that it were as easy as the way you want, but I don't believe that it will be, especially when the judge sees that you have changed attorneys. They will remember your case very easily because the first time you went to court, Attorney Manti represented you. Believe me, everyone in the judicial system knows him. This puts me in a very delicate situation. I hope for the best!!!

**Mrs. Dion:** I understand that Attorney Manti is one of your Illustrious friends, but I believe that you will do just fine in the name of the judicial system. After you see what I've got to show you. I will be very confident in your work. (She opens her purse and takes out a few pictures and gives them to the attorney.) Look at this! My husband in the arms of another woman. Please, look at this woman very closely and tell me if you recognize her. And this is the reason why the judge said the proof was insufficient to give me a legal separation!!!

**Attorney:** (Gets the pictures from Mrs. Dion and starts to look at them closely.) No!!! This is not possible. I can't believe what I seeing in these pictures. It can't be true. Do you know who this woman is? Am I stupid or what? Yes, I am stupid to believe everything she told me!!! This is my wife. You understand, this is my wife. My wife betrayed me with your husband. Please do not say anything. I have to collect myself. I am lost!!!

**Mrs. Dion:** I know the way you feel. You still think that this is not enough proof to ask for a separation or divorce. When I found out about this, I went crazy. . . .

**Attorney:** Oh!!! Now everything changes. Now that we have all the papers on the table, it is very clear that you want justice. I still do not believe what I see in these pictures. I do not deserve that. I do not deserve that!!!

**Mrs. Dion:** I hope that now you will persuade the judge. We do not deserve to be betrayed!!!

**Attorney:** I will destroy your husband! He will regret being born into this world. When I am finished with the legal action, I will personally confront him. He is a miserable no-good and does not respect our friendship. How could he betray a beautiful lady like you? I do not understand what kind of man this guy is!!! I will take care of my wife too. She is a no-good selfish woman. I never betrayed her. I have had a lot of opportunity, but never in my life have I betrayed her.

**Mrs. Dion:** Do you understand now the way you feel when you have been betrayed by the person whom you love, by the person whom you give your soul, by the person whom you trusted? Do you realize that every night I get undressed in front of this person to give the best of me and this is what I get!?! It's betrayal. It is best I stop talking now before I go into his office and do something that I will regret later!!!

**Attorney:** I will try to comfort you!!! I now know the way people feel when they ask for a divorce. In this moment I have to stay calm. I have to be patient. I do not want to do anything stupid. I have to keep my feelings inside of me!!!

**Mrs:** Dion: I understand!!! I understand very well!!!

**Attorney:** I ask for your forgiveness. I never would have imagined this happening. I am sorry for my stupidity in questioning you!!! Now we have to do what we have to do to punish these two people. We have to be avenged for the way these people made us suffer. Tomorrow I will start to study this case intensely. Please, if you have any papers at home regarding this case, bring them over!!!

**Mrs. Dion:** Do not worry. I will assist you with everything you need. I will bring you the files that I have at home. We have to get our revenge.

**Attorney:** If you like I can pass by your home and pick up all of the paperwork that you have regarding this case. Tell me, what time will you be home tomorrow?

**Mrs. Dion:** You're coming to my house!!! No, you can't do that. I can't have you come into my home. You cannot imagine the way my husband acts when I invite someone into the house.

**Attorney:** Don't tell me your husband is jealous. After what he did to both of us? I think this is a good excuse for me to be in your house just in case he comes home from the office and finds me there. I would love to start making this man very miserable.

**Mrs. Dion:** I would love for you to do whatever you think is right to have your revenge, but the man is crazy. Since I have asked for a divorce, he has been acting differently. I don't want anything to happen to you. We have to work on this matter slowly. You can't imagine how I would love to make this man miserable, but I have to protect my integrity for now. Also, I don't want anything to happen to you.

**Attorney:** I personally think that if he saw his wife in someone else's arms, he would realize what he did wrong and this would be the start of the revenge!!!

**Mrs. Dion:** Please!!! Let's be calm in this situation. Let's use our heads. We can't do what we would like to do. We have to follow the law. Otherwise, we will be guilty instead.

**Attorney:** I do not know why you are so protective of him. Wouldn't you like to do him what he has done to you? Maybe you will give him the reason that you would forgive him.

**Mrs. Dion:** I can't believe you mention the word forgive. I detest this man, you understand that!!! I detest him with passion. (Someone knocks on the door.)

**Attorney:** Please, Mrs. Dion, let me see who this is. (Looks at his watch.) Oh, I almost forgot. I have another appointment.

(Goes to the door to see who is knocking.)

**Mrs. Dion:** (With frightened look on her face.) Maybe it is my husband. Sometimes he follows me or maybe someone who saw me coming here called him.

**Attorney:** Be calm, Mrs. Dion. You are in a law office. I don't think that your husband would be so stupid as to come here. I can give him a lot of trouble. If you are really scared, I can let you go into the other room that connects to my home. I do not know if my wife is home, but I'm sure she won't say anything.

**Mrs. Dion:** Yes!!! Maybe you are right!!! I should go into the other room. If I see your wife, I will be very polite to her, but in reality, I would love to kill her, but!!!

(The attorney looks through a crack in the door that leads into his house. At the same time the housekeeper opens the door of the office to tell the attorney that Mr. Sal Corini is in the waiting room.)

**Attorney:** (To the housekeeper.) Diane, please take Mrs. Dion into the other room!!!

**Diane:** Mrs. Dion, please follow me!!! (They exit.)

**Attorney:** (Tries to put some of his paperwork in order and talks to himself.) Ah!!! If she was single and her father was not my friend, I would love to spend some time with her. She is so beautiful and we both have been betrayed. (The telephone rings.) Hello!!! Who!?! The Attorney Conti!?! Oh, he just stepped out for a moment. I will tell him to call you back!!! Where is my secretary when I need her!?! I have to let go, I can't work like this. (The phone rings again.) (He lets it ring a few times, then he disconnects it.) Damn it. Today of all days, she has to take the day off. How can I help other people when I can't even help myself? (He goes toward the door that opens into his office.) Please, Mr. Corini, come in!!! I apologize for making you wait!!!

**Sal:** Please call me Sal, we are friends. How are you doing? The last time I saw you was at the wedding. How is everything going?

**Attorney:** Sal my dear friend, what can I do for you? I thought you were in Paris for a change of atmosphere after you broke up with Pamela. Maybe you need fresh air or the beautiful girls of Paris to help you forget. You are a lucky man. You do not have to work for a living. You have the money and you can do whatever you like, go anyplace you like. You do not have to answer to anyone about your actions, not like me who has to ask my stupid wife every time I take a step!!!

**Sal:** I can't believe you just said that!!! If I had a wife like yours, I would stay at home day and night. Do not be jealous of my lifestyle. Sometimes I would love to have a beautiful wife to come home to!!!

**Attorney:** It is nice to see you again. Now tell me this is a visit to an old friend or do I have to help you in a legal matter, tell me!!!

**Sal:** I am here for a legal question but more than that to be a friend when you answer my question. Please, use your best ability as an attorney.

**Attorney:** Please tell me, tell me the ideas that are in your head. I will try to help you out but please hurry, I am waiting for Mr. Bardi and his wife. I don't know why, they just told me that it was urgent, that they speak with me and I had to see them as soon as possible.

**Sal:** Ah!!! I am so happy, very happy. I started to believe that maybe Pamela, that beautiful Pamela, could be mine. I do believe in miracles!!!

**Attorney:** (Interrupts Sal.) Please, tell me!!! Don't tell me that she betrayed her husband already!!! She just got married and they are still on their honeymoon!!! I didn't think that this would happen so soon. I do not want to believe that in Paris you did the impossible. Tell me!!! Tell me!!!

**Sal:** I would like to tell you everything that happened in Paris, but it would take a lot of your time. Let's just say that I have a good feeling that Pamela will be back with me soon.

**Attorney:** In the beginning everybody thought that you and Pamela would be husband and wife after you broke up with Teresa, who I think is a beautiful woman.

**Sal:** Teresa will always be in my heart. I can't forget her and, yes, she is a very beautiful lady. I thought that I would marry her, but ever since the day she introduced me to Pamela, my feelings just changed. Pamela gave me such a shock. My body and my mind were paralyzed at the sight of her. I would do anything to be with her.

**Attorney:** I think I know the way you feel, but tell me, what do I have to do with your feelings for Pamela?

**Sal:** Oh!!! You can do!!! You can do everything in your power to help me fulfill my dream. You have to help me get Pamela to divorce her husband. I will pay any amount of money to ensure that she gets a divorce. I want to be her husband and I want to marry her.

**Attorney:** Take it easy, my friend. I think you're going too fast. Before anything happens; I will have to talk to Pamela. The situation is not as easy as you think. If I can help you I will, but the law is clear. Before any divorce goes through, there has to be a meeting of reconciliation between husband and wife. Also, don't forget that I am a friend of the family and I have to do everything in my power to save that marriage. I believe that Greg is in love with his wife and they look very good together.

**Sal:** What am I asking you, my dear friend, is to make Pamela feel comfortable when she asks you about the consequences of having a divorce. Remember also that I am your friend and the way that I feel about Pamela.

**Attorney:** I understand!!! I understand, my dear friend, but our friendship has nothing to do with the way you follow the law. I'll tell you now that I will try everything in my power to keep these two together and I do believe that Pamela and Greg should have another chance to be together for life.

(Someone knocks on the door. It's Diane, the housekeeper.)

**Diane:** Can I come in?

**Attorney:** Yes, come in. What do you want now?

**Diane:** Your wife is not home and I just wanted to let you know that Mrs. Dion started to feel dizzy, so I told her to lie on the sofa. I am going to go to the pharmacy to get some medicine.

**Attorney:** I hope it is nothing serious, but it is a good idea. Ask the pharmacist to give you something to help her. Please do not stay out too long. (The bell rings.)

**Diane:** Right away!!!

**Attorney:** What a day. I do not even have time to go to the bathroom!!!

**Diane:** It is Miss Pamela Bard.

**Sal:** Pamela is here? Please tell her to come in, please!!!

**Attorney:** Let her come in.

(Opens the door.) Please come in, Miss Bard.

**Attorney:** (To Diane.) Please go now and I recommend that you don't take long. (Pamela enters.)

**Diane:** Don't worry. I'll be back as fast as I can. (She leaves the stage.)

**Attorney:** Mrs. Pite!!! How is everything? Please, sit down.

**Pamela:** Miss!!! Please if you do not mind!!!

**Sal:** Oh, Pamela!!! My dear Pamela, how are you doing?

**Pamela:** Hi, Sal!!! I am fine. How are you doing?

**Sal:** I am so pleased to see you again. After all of my suffering, it is a miracle to see you. This is the best gift you could give me. I

**can't** believe that he did what he did. He doesn't merit a wife like you. You deserve better. He betrayed you, I still can't believe it!!!

**Attorney:** Please, Sal, please!!! (To Pamela.) Do not listen to what he is saying. Please, Sal, if we are finished talking, I would like a few minutes with Pamela!!!

**Pamela:** Thank you!!! Thank you very much, Attorney Conti!!! (Toward Sal.) I would like to tell you that Greg never betrayed me, and please stop telling people that Greg was with another woman when we were on our honeymoon!!!

**Sal:** I never tell lies. I tell what I see and to be precise, you saw Greg with your own eyes what he did in Paris. I don't understand what you see in a man like that and why you got married to him.

**Pamela:** I know I saw him, but he gave me an explanation. I believe him but what happened in Paris hurt me very much. I have to make a decision and I do not need your help to do that.

**Sal:** You do what you think is right for you. Maybe the attorney can help you with your decision. You know that I love you and I will do anything to have you back, but you are the one who has to decide what is best for you. Your happiness is mine and I am sure that our friend here will give you the best advice to resolve this matter.

**Attorney:** Dear friend, this is not Paris, this is America. The laws are different here. Matrimony is not easy to break even with divorce. I see that every time I go to court.

**Sal:** (Toward Pamela.) I told you to stay in Paris. Everything would be easy, especially divorce.

**Pamela:** I talked to my parents and they thought that I should come back to America and resolve the problem here. I am sure that everything will be fine. Greg knows that I came here and I am sure he will come here to talk. (Someone knocks on the door of the office.)

**Attorney:** I am sorry but my secretary tool the day off today and besides being an attorney, I have to answer the door too. I am

**sorry** for the interruption. (Goes to the door to see who it is.)

**Sal:** (To the attorney.) Please, if it is Greg, it is better if he doesn't see me here. I wouldn't want to make a scene in your office. I am sure that at this moment his mind id very confused about everything that has happened.

**Attorney:** I think that's a good idea. If it is Greg, you can go out the door. (He points to the door that leads into his house. He walks to the door of the studio to see who is knocking at the door. It is Greg with his mother-in-law and father-in-law. The attorney leaves the office and starts to talk with them in the waiting room. He leaves the door to the office partially open so that Pamela and Sal can hear them talking.)

**Pamela:** (Gets up and goes to the door of the office to see with her own eyes what is going on. She turns toward Sal.) You are not a man who can stand up in a troubled situation. You see, right now I'd like you to stay here as a friend and show me the character of man or be by my side when Greg gets here. I am so confused.

**Sal:** My dear Pamela, you know that for you I would do the

**impossible,** but you have to understand that it is not my place to be here and defend you from circumstances caused by your husband. Sorry, Greg knows our past relationship and he would be suspicious if he sees me here. Also, you have to understand that we are in the office of an attorney and I don't want to make a scene. You know that fighting is not my nature, I am a lover, not a fighter!!!

**Pamela:** In that case it is better if you leave by way of the attorney's house. You are a coward, not a man!!! Please go!!! Go!!!

**Sal:** (In an aside.) It is stupid to stay here and fight or be part of some reconciliation. I hope they get divorced. (Sal gets up and goes out the door that joins the studio to the house.)

**Attorney:** (Enters the studio with Lio, Sue, and Greg.) (To Pamela.) Please, Pamela, let's be realistic. We have to talk about this situation like mature adults. (Toward Sal, Lio, and Greg.) Please sit down!!!

**Pamela:** You do not lose a minute. You follow me all over!!!

**Attorney:** Please, Mrs. Pite!! Please!!! Do not start!!!

**Sue:** (To Pamela.) That is the reason you went out this morning—to come here!!!

**Greg:** (To Pamela.) How soon we change feelings. You can't even look at me in the face. Don't forget that I am still your husband. Don't you ever forget that.

**Pamela:** What do you want me to say? I never expected you to be a traitor, to betray me. I never expected that!!!

**Lio:** My dear daughter, please calm down. Greg told me everything that happened that night. We had been set up by someone, and believe me, I will find out. You can't believe that I would betray your mother or that Greg would betray you. He loves you and you know it!!!

**Sue:** Listen to your father. I forgive him for whatever happened in Paris. Listen!!!

**Attorney:** Please, my dear friends, I talk to you all as my friends. I personally think that we can get to a reasonable solution to this situation. You two are young, you can have a great future together. It would be very sad for me to take sides with either of you two. You are still newlyweds; everything will be fine. You are made for each other!!! You can talk about divorce or separation. In this moment it is just that Pamela is very upset because of what has happened.

**Greg:** Listen to our friend, my love. He knows best, he is an attorney. At this moment we should be on our honeymoon and instead we are here talking about divorce.

**Attorney:** Greg, you are right!!! This is wrong that you two are here. You should be having the best times of your life right now!!! This is not right!!!

**Pamela:** Are all of you trying to tell me to forget about what happened in Paris? He betrayed me. Do you understand that he betrayed me before I could even sleep with him and become his wife!!!

**Sue:** Pamela!!! Please, Pamela, don't use the word betray so easily.

 **Did** you see Greg in bed with anyone else? He just hugged that girl he thought was a fan. Nothing more!!!

**Attorney:** Listen!!! If you like, we can start all over again. Pamela, please explain why you want to get a divorce or separation so fast. I am listening!!!

**Pamela:** I do not know. I am so confused!!! Separation!!! Divorce!!! I don't know!!!

**Lio:** (Joking.) Paris, what a city. Freedom!!! Oh, Paris, I miss you!!!

**Sue:** If this is the way you approach this problem, then I am with my daughter and I will refuse to live the rest of my life with you. If you think that this is just nothing for a man to betray his wife, I and Pamela refuse this condition!!!

**Pamela:** I agree with my mother. This is not the right way to treat a wife!!!

**Lio:** I was just joking. You women take everything so seriously!!!

**Greg:** Please, Lio. I am not joking. This is a serious situation for me.

**Attorney:** Please, gentlemen, please calm down. I don't understand anything that is going on. Please.

**Sue:** I can't speak for you, Pamela, but I think I should teach a lesson to my dear husband. (To her husband.) If you think you can find happiness in Paris, then go because I am very serious about a separation from you!!!

**Pamela:** Oh, Mother!!! You are so strong mentally. I agree with you. We should teach these men a lesson. Separation it is!!!

**Attorney:** Calm!!! Please calm down. Do you people know what a separation is? This is not a joking situation and I am in the middle. This is nothing to laugh about. Let me explain what a legal separation is. First you have to act like civil people, no fighting. You two must have complaints with good reason before the judge will even consider a separation. The way that I see it, it would be difficult for Greg and Pamela to get a separation.

**Pamela:** I can't believe you're telling me this. I do not see anything difficult in this matter right now. Greg is my husband on paper. We never consummated our rite of husband and wife. I am still a virgin.

**Greg:** I am ready to fulfill my obligation as a husband, but you never gave me the opportunity to do so!!!

**Pamela:** You're right!!! And I am glad that I never did. I do not want to be your wife.

**Attorney:** I think that you two have a serious problem and I personally can resolve that, but do not forget that in order to have the separation and then to nullify the marriage, both of you have to get some consent.

**Sue:** I think they will have no problem with that. Separation will be the only solution.

**Pamela:** I agree with mother. The separation is the only solution!!!

**Lio:** If this is what my wife wants, I have no problem with it. I will give her the separation, but I want to be clear that I never did anything to deserve this. I have always followed the rules of being a married man, and I never betrayed my wife in any way. (To Sue.) You can break up this marriage after so many years, but think hard before going through with this separation before it's too late!!!

**Greg:** I do not agree with that!!! I do not want a separation. I want to be married to the one I love even if it takes some time for her to forgive me. my wife cannot leave me for a sin that I never committed. This is not right!!! Please, dear attorney, tell her that; she can't leave the house that was built for all of us!!!

**Pamela:** Let's be precise here. I never abandoned any house. We never lived in any house. Yes, we built it and it should have been our future home, but I never!!! (To the attorney.) If I were an attorney, I would not even mention the word abandon!!!

**Attorney:** Please, Pamela!!! Maybe I misunderstand, but it seems like you refused to follow your husband after the two of you got married. This is not right and the judge will take that into consideration. This will be in your husband's favor!!!

**Sue:** (In a loud voice.) You are trying to tell me that our husbands can do whatever they want to do and we have to accept it without saying anything? Oh no, my dear friend!!!

**Pamela:** I saw my husband in someone else's arms, hugging and kissing, and I should just let that go like nothing happened? What am I supposed to do, just stay there and watch? Maybe tell them to go ahead and finish the act by making love. Please don't tell me that I am wrong.

**Attorney:** I never said that you were wrong about what happened in Paris. I just said that you should have followed your husband into the new house, talked about what happened, and then pursued the legal matters!!!

**Pamela:** My dear attorney, the reason why I did not follow him to our new house is because I did not forgive him for what he did. Every time I looked at him, I saw the other woman in his arms. It is very hard for me to forget so soon. I hope you understand what I am saying!!!

**Lio:** (To attorney.) Listen, my friend, everything that my daughter and my wife are telling you is not the truth. Nobody here betrayed anyone. I think that the air in Paris made my wife and my daughter sick. I am sure that they need some help!!!

**Sue:** We were betrayed!!! You two are going to pay for that. These are my last words, like it or not!!!

**Pamela:** Dad!!! Why don't you admit that you two made a terrible mistake to leave us by ourselves in Paris and try to have an affair? Even if it was just for a few hours with an easy catch. (In a rising voice.) And you, Greg, I do not understand what you want to do, just practice a little before making love to me?

**Attorney:** Please, Mrs. Pite, calm. Don't raise your voice. Be calm and we can come to a conclusion. I suggest that Mrs. Pite!!!

**Pamela:** (Interrupts the attorney.) Miss!!! Please!!!

**Attorney:** (To Pamela.) Oh!!! Miss!!! Mrs.!!! I am starting to lose my patience and I don't understand anything anymore. You gentlemen are driving me crazy. My office is not a court room. I

**am** just trying to make the peace between you all. The judge in the court will have to decide the final conclusion to your problem!!!

**Lio:** (To Pamela, Greg, and his wife.) Please all of you, silence. This will be the last time I will explain what happened to the attorney. After that we can go to court or whatever!!!

**Sue:** You have nothing to explain. The attorney is just trying to make things easier for you and Greg. (To the attorney.) Dear attorney, I saw my husband go into a séparé where a beautiful young lady was waiting, I went to see what was going on and I saw my husband and the naked lady!!!

**Lio:** Yes, you have all the right in the world to be mad, but I was there just looking at her. I never did anything to hurt you and you know that!!!

**Pamela:** My husband instead was embracing this beautiful lady and giving her a passionate kiss.

**Greg:** I was not kissing her. She gave me a kiss for good luck on my

**career** as a player!!

**Attorney:** Do you ladies have proof of what happened? We can prove it in court that whatever you say is true. Do you have some pictures, a witness?

**Pamela:** What picture? What witness? You don't believe what we have told you? My word is more proof than some pictures or any witness you could find!!!

**Attorney:** Calm down, Miss!!! Calm!!! I did believe you all, but remember that it is the judge that you have to convince, not me. He will want proof. Just proof can make this case easy!!!

**Lio:** Our ladies can't prove anything because there is nothing to prove. It was a stupid moment of weakness. We did nothing wrong!!!

**Sue:** Oh!!! Just a few moments of weakness. I can bet that if I never went looking for him, there would have been more than a few moments of weakness with that young lady!!!

**Pamela:** Oh!!! My husband just kissing!!! I could tell that he already started to get tired of my kiss. It was so passionate that if I didn't stop him, it probably would have been more than a kiss!!!

**Greg:** Hell to the game!!! Hel to the soccer!!! It is not my fault I have so many fans and the majority of them are women!!!

**Pamela:** But the kiss!!! Fan or no fans, you have to understand that you are married!!!

**Attorney:** Please, do not interrupt. I insist (To Lio.) Please continue to talk!!!

**Lio:** Oh!!! Where was I!?! Oh!!! After what I already told you, my wife and my daughter came back to America and came to see you and let's be precise that when my wife got home, she prohibited me from sleeping in the bedroom. I would like to say that the bedroom is also where I keep all of my clothes!!!

**Sue:** And I would like to remind you that you will never be sleeping in the bedroom with me again!!!

**Greg:** My wife refused to follow me into our new house that I prepared for the rest of our lives together!!!

**Pamela:** I was dreaming about that too, but I never thought that my Husband would betray me!!!

**Attorney:** Please calm down!!! There is too much confusion!!! I can't concentrate!!!

**Lio:** I can't believe that after one day of being back from Paris my wife made an appointment with you.

**Greg:** (Interrupts.) Like you heard, dear attorney, our wives do not follow their husbands and forgive for any mistakes, but the husbands have to follow the wife if something happens and we have to forgive them.

**Pamela:** I can't believe that you still talk!!! Don't forget that on the day I was supposedly your wife, you were about to go to bed with another woman. Don't tell me you forgot her name already!!! Well, I will remind you of it!!! Does Renee sound familiar? I see that woman every time I look at you. I will never forget her.

**Sue:** (To Lio.) And you!!! What a good example. You are the one who provoked all of this scandal and you have the remorse over creating the unhappiness that will haunt your daughter for the rest of her life!!!

**Greg:** (To Pamela.) I would like to justify my act, not just with words, but with my heart. I would like to make you understand that what happened in Paris was not my fault.

**Pamela:** (To Greg.) You have nothing to justify. You are guilty. I caught you committing the act!!! Go back to Renee!!!

**Greg:** (To the attorney.) What Pamela is saying is the truth, but she never gave me the opportunity to explain myself. That lady who hugged and kissed me in Paris was a fan. I never saw that lady before in my life. I am an athlete who plays sports, and like any other athlete, I am loved by millions of fans. Sometimes acts like the one that happened in Paris you can't stop or avoid especially if the team wins.

**Pamela:** Do not believe what he is saying, my dear attorney, because when I went to see the séparé where Renee was at the table fixed for two people, candles were lit. That tells me that everything was set up for a lovely dinner. I can't believe that if you love someone, nobody, not even a famous soccer player like Greg would have accepted.

**Greg:** Please stop!!! Do not say such stupid words. Do not say that I don't love you because of what happened!!! You know that I love you and that's why I married you. I will sooner or later make you believe that I will always love you with my heart.

**Pamela:** It took just a caress. A kiss from a fan, like you say, to make you forget that you were married. That your wife traveled a long distance just to be next to you. Win or lose I was there for you. If anyone would have come to me and kissed me for any reason, I would have slapped them. I believe that you could have kept Rachael away from you if you wanted to!!!

**Greg:** But!!! Rachael!!!

**Pamela:** (Interrupts Greg.) Listen, my dear attorney!!! Listen!!! He pronounces the name Rachael with so much passion. I'm starting to get sick!!! I do not want to listen to any more excuses, please!!! I want the separation. Do you understand that!!!

**Greg:** The only reason I know her name is because you have repeated it a million times. That lady did not kiss me because I am a man; she kissed me out of infatuation that she has toward the athlete that is in every newspaper around the world. This happens every day. An athlete is recognized for his talent more than anything else. I would think that you would be a happy wife seeing your husband on the front page of the newspaper.

**Pamela:** You are going to insinuate that you never met Renee before?

**Greg:** I swear on the sacred sacrament of our wedding that I never meant to hurt you in any way!!! I love you!!!

**Pamela:** Please!!! Do not swear on the sacrament. It is a very serious offense toward God.

**Greg:** Tell me!!! Tell everyone in this room why I got married to you. If it was not love, what for? If I wanted to be a Casanova and go to bed with any girl who liked me, I would have done that. I am not interested in any other girl or woman. I chose you to give all of my love to for eternity. You are the only woman I love. You are in my heart every moment of the day. No other women mean anything to me. You have to trust me. Please give me another chance to prove my love to you and that I have told the truth about Paris.

**Attorney:** Listen, everybody!!! Please listen. I am sorry to interrupt this meeting or argument, whatever you want to call it, but I can't listen any longer. I have things to do. Please try to resolve this matter in a civil way. I can just tell you to analyze the case and find a way to reconcile. First put everything out and then let your hearts talk. (The bell rings.) Excuse me, I have to go see who that is. (Exits.)

**Lio:** I personally think the attorney is right!!! We can try to resolve this matter on our own terms. Try!!!

**Greg:** I think my father-in-law is right!!!

**(The** attorney enters the office with Teresa.)

**Teresa:** Hi, everyone!!! I knew I would find you all here!!! Please, all of you, listen to me. I would like to tell you the story about all of this mess. As everyone knows, I was in Paris when everything started. I was a witness to this matter. I would like for you all to listen and then we can make peace between you all. It is your option, but I will try my best.

**Sue:** What peace? We want to avenge ourselves!!!

**Attorney:** Please!!! Stay calm. I would like to listen to what Teresa has to say about this matter.

**Teresa:** Well, everyone in this place knows that Sal is still in love with Pamela. He never will accept the fact that Pamela married Greg. Sal planned everything that happened in Paris. He paid Renee and Rachael to play a part in this plot. He wants to see Pamela and Greg get a divorce because he is in love. Do not forget that love can make a man do strange things. I am with you all; what Sal did is not right. That's the reason I came forward to tell you all what happened in Paris. Now it's up to you to figure out the solution. I believe that you all can make a good family. At one time I liked Greg myself, but if he chose Pamela instead, it is because he loves her. This is the only thing I have to say.

**Attorney:** Thank you!!! Thank you for coming forward and trying to resolve this matter.

**Greg:** Thank you, Teresa. Thank you very much. I hope that Pamela will now believe me that I never intended to hurt her or betray her with another woman. (To Pamela.) You, my dear Pam, do not want to listen to me when I have been trying to tell you the truth. I would have done the same. You were very insulted and upset and I sympathize with you. I almost lost you for a crime I never committed. Just remember the time we were engaged and you should understand the love that I have for you. We need to just have our eyes look at each other and no words to understand that we are made for each other. (Greg gets close to Pamela, gets her hands and kisses them again.) Lot of happy hours!!! Don't tell me that you forgot the long walk in the woods. We wrote our names on every tree, we planted seed, we had lunch sitting at the big stone looking onto the little brook with water so limp. We sat and talked about our future, to get married and have our own house. I still remember all the kisses we shared when I asked you to be my wife. You were so happy and excited that we almost made love in the woods. We stopped before doing so because we didn't want to break the promise to make love the day that we were married. I could have made love to you if I didn't love you with my heart, but instead I waited till the day you became my wife. Do you remember?

**Pamela:** And now that I am your wife, it took just a few days to forget all the promises that you made, all the love that you promised.

**Greg:** Please, Pamela, don't start again. You know that I did nothing wrong. That lady who kissed me was paid to do so. You heard what Teresa said. It was set up by your old boyfriend.

**Pamela:** You are so stupid. He never was my boyfriend!!!

**Greg:** Thank you. I deserve that!!! If you think that I tried to betray

**you!!!** (The attorney walks through the office and starts talking to himself softly.)

**Pamela:** I just said that you disappoint me. I was so excited to be your wife. I don't care that you are famous, but I can't stand it when another woman puts her hands on you!!!

**Attorney:** The agitated sea!!! The boat!!!

**Lio:** What the hell are you talking about? The boat!!! The sea!!! I don't understand!!!

**Attorney:** (To Greg.) You are guilty of telling the truth!!!

**Greg:** Yes!!! I told you that I am guilty of being honest. You know what happened in Paris.

**Pamela:** The truth!!! The real truth, confess!!!

**Greg:** I confess!!! I confess!!! The lady got me unexpectedly and kissed me just like that. (He suddenly gets Pamela in his arms and kisses her.) Do you see? I kissed you unexpectedly. You are a victim like I was in Paris. Do you believe me, now you do!!! (The room is very silent. Pamela is astonished; she gets close and gets close and kisses Greg. He touches her face gently.) Please let me hear you voice in a gentle way. The way it was before all of this happened. I just want to understand that I love you and nothing else counts. (Suddenly the door of the office opens. The housekeeper follows a very elegant gentleman.)

**Mr.** Dion: (With a baritone voice.) My wife is here?

**Attorney:** You!!! You!!! What are you doing in my studio?

**Mr.** Dion: I don't see her!!! Where is she? Where is my wife? (He raises the cane in a daggerlike way.)

**Housekeeper:** (Gets scared.) She is in the other room. (She points to the door that connects to the attorney's house. The attorney gives her a dirty look.)

**Mr.** Dion: My wife is in your house!!! What is she doing in your house? (He gets close to the door and opens it violently.)

**Scene:** (Mrs. Dion is relaxing on the sofa. Sal kneels on the floor next to the sofa to hold her hand. When Mrs. Dion (half-awake) sees her husband, she hugs Sal.)

**Mr.** Dion: I caught you!!!

**Mrs. Dion:** Yes, you caught me. Now you can see that I have a lover just like you. At least someone appreciates me. You thought you were the only one doing the betraying. (She exits.)

**Mr.** Dion: (In a dangerous way, he raises his cane.) You!!! You!!!!

Do not think that this is the end. You will see how far I can go!!!

**Sal:** You think what you want, but you don't scare me. I am ready for any action you take.

**Attorney:** (Who was next to the door and observed everything that was going on in his house. Points toward Sal.) I knew you would avenge your friend!!!

**Mr.** Dion: This is not the end!!! Good-bye, everyone, good-bye. (Turns toward Sal.) You can expect whatever. Your life will be full of surprises, just watch yourself. (Exits.)

**Pamela:** (To Sal.) You deserve that!!! I hope that he will hurt you for good because if he doesn't hurt you, I will!!!

**Greg:** (Gets close to Pamela and stands next to the door of the attorney's house.) She is right. You are a vile creature. I would like to put my hands on you!!! (Pamela kisses him.)

**Lio:** You really deserve a lesson. (Gets close to his wife and kisses her.)

**Sue:** Do you think that I have forgotten what you did in Paris? But I still love you after all these years.

**Greg:** I finally feel good about all of this and that I can show you my innocence. Now tell me why kissed me?

**Pamela:** You're asking me why? Why!!! It is because I love you. (They hug again and kiss each other.)

**Greg:** Now I will take you away from here. You will never escape from my love. You never will be away from my heart till the end of my days. (Gets Pamela in his arms and next to the door of the

**studio.** He turns toward everyone and says:) We will go to an unknown location, so please do not look for us. (Exits.)

**Sal:** I lost her!!! I lost her for good. I don't know what I will do now. Everyone is against me now!!!

**Sue:** What is going on? My daughter leaves without saying good-bye. I do not understand!!!

**Lio:** Good!!! Very good! I am so happy. I was waiting for you to see that I am so happy!!!

**Sue:** Go away without saying good-bye. I do not accept that. I am sure that they will go home to get the suitcase. I would like to say a few words to my son-in-law. He does not know me very well, but I will make sure that he will. I am going. Good-bye, everyone. (Exits.)

**Lio:** Like you see, my dear attorney, my wife is the boss and she thinks the way she wants to think. I will follow her before she makes any more trouble.

**Attorney:** I agree with you. Try to catch up with her and give her a kiss for forgiveness for what happened in Paris.

**Lio:** I do not really think that my kiss will make her forget!!! (Exits.)

**Attorney:** (To Sal and Teresa.) You two can stay here. I have to go, I am late. What a day!!! (Exits.)

**Sal:** (Puts his hands on his face.) I don't know!!! I don't know!!!

**Teresa:** You don't know what? Tell me!!! I think you deserve every punishment that you get, my dear Giovanni. I do not understand what you were doing kneeling down next to Mrs. Dion. Honestly, I do not want to know!!! I just know that you aren't her lover!!!

**Sal:** Thank you. Thank you for believing in me. I was holding her hand because she was sick and I was just trying to comfort her, nothing more.

**Teresa:** I do not care what you were doing!!!

**Sal:** I hope you forgive me. Everyone else wants to punish me and I

**don't** know why. What I did was for love and nothing more!!!

**Teresa:** Now you are scared. I hope you learned your lesson. What were you thinking?

**Sal:** I just wanted to say that Greg is a lucky man.

**Teresa:** Do not talk about Greg. He is a real man who stands for what he believes in. He is a man and I wish him and Pamela all the luck in the world. I wish he will go as high as he can with his profession of soccer. He deserves the best.

**Sal:** If this is your wish, I will not argue about it. I hope that you get your wish!!!

**Teresa:** I know in my heart that he is a very gentle man. I do not have to wish him anything!!!

**Sal:** Finally, why won't you tell me why you like him? Please, tell me. Do you like to make me jealous? I am not, I am who I am and never will change.

**Teresa:** After what happened in Paris, nobody trusts you. All of your friends will hate you unless I reconcile you with everyone for your own good.

**Sal:** You are saying that you will do that for me? I do not know how to thank you!!! I will be saved from the hate that everyone has for me.

**Teresa:** I think everyone will forget you one way or the other because they will understand that what you did was out of love.

**Sal:** (Gets close to Teresa and gets her hand.) Please forgive me for what I have done. You are a good person, too good for me. I would like to forget everything and start a new life, be a better person. I would like for you to be my wife!!!

**Teresa:** Please do not kid me. This is a serious proposition. Do not forget that I am a woman with integrity. Yes, I love you and a proposal like the one you just made I can accept if you would love me the way that I love you.

**Sal:** (Gets close to Teresa and hugs and kisses her.) Believe it or not, I still love you!!!

**Attorney:** (Enters the studio and sees Teresa and Sal embraced.) Excuse me!!! Oh, I am so happy that everyone is starting to understand that the best medicine is happiness. I am so happy. I wonder when I will be so happy. I have to make my marriage work somehow!!!

**Sal:** This is the first time that I have started to feel good about myself, like a real man. (Gets close to Teresa and kisses her, caressing her cheek.) You make me so happy!!! I feel like a real man!!! Thank you!!!

The End!

**ADOLFO RUDY GELSI** graduated from engineering school in his native Italy and aviation school in the I.S., where he employed his skills as an aviation technician before retiring because of a disability.

The author now devotes his time to writing drama, poetry, and short stories. His work has appeared in the newspaper of his residence in Connecticut.

When a young woman named Pamela, the light of Sal Corini's life, dedicates her youth and beauty in marriage to a rising young soccer star, the rebuffed older man begins to act like Shakespeare's Iago. Vowing not to be the loser, Sal begins to mix potent cocktails of jealousy and unscrupulous behavior, served to more people than just the bride and groom. Fate lends a hand just before the wedding, calling Greg unexpectedly to play in the World Cup in Paris.

Who will have the last laugh in this dramatic comedy of innuendo? With five people clamoring for divorce, whose is not granted.